Hot Lesbian Erotica

I0683469

Catfight, Climax, Friends Again

by. Miranda Mars

The Laura and
Shontay Chronicles **Part 2**

About the Publisher

4Fun Publishing, a member of **BLVNP Incorporated**, 340 S. Lemon #6200, Walnut CA 91789, info@blvnp.com / legal@blvnp.com
NOTE: Due to the highly emotional reaction of some people to works of erotic fiction, any email sent to the above address that contains foul language or religious references is automatically deleted by our anti-spam software and will not be seen. All other communications are welcome.

DISCLAIMER

Please don't be stupid and kill yourself. This book is a work of FICTION. Do not try any new sexual practice that you find in this book. It is fiction and not to be confused with reality. Neither the author nor the publisher or its associates assume any responsibility for any loss, injury, death or legal consequences resulting from acting on the contents in this book. Every character in this book is over 18 years of age. The author's opinions are not to be construed as the opinions of the publisher. The material in this book is for entertainment purposes ONLY. Enjoy.

The Laura and Shontay Chronicles, Part 2

Catfight, Climax, Friends Again

Hot Lesbian Erotica

By: Miranda Mars

ISBN: 978-1-68030-317-9

Laura heard something upstairs.

She knew the Gibsons were gone since she had seen them out the window as they were leaving earlier that day, getting into an airport shuttle with several pieces of luggage. That could mean only one thing: Shontay. When her folks were gone, she came over to feed their cat Willie and spend a little time with him. She was up there. She should've taken off her shoes, if she didn't want me to hear her, Laura thought. Maybe she doesn't realize how these old apartments telegraph every little thing.

Shontay still had not phoned Laura. Let's see, it must be almost ten days or so since she called, Laura thought, counting back. Very odd. Something's going on. They told her about the screaming and groaning down here, I'll bet, she thought, glumly.

Laura had been in such a flutter of love and exuberant sexual happiness following her night with Sara that almost nothing else had got her attention for days. On top of that, she had engaged a real estate person—a friend of Rhonda's—who had within days found her a delightful condo nestled in a forested slope on the western side of the lower Twin Peaks area. It was heavily wooded and could be foggy at times, but it was fairly new, only one previous owner, and secure and private.

Laura had made clear to the agent that, as she had put it, she couldn't bear listening to other people's noises, dogs, odious rock music, quarrels, and that that was the reason she was moving in the first place. They performed, with the cooperation of Laura's potential neighbors, several experiments to detect how soundproof these condos were, and Laura was tickled to find that someone playing heavy metal at an ear-shattering volume directly next door might as well be on the moon.

"You could commit murder in here and never be discovered until the smells started emanating," the real estate guy, a dour old man with a huge distended belly and rheumy yellow eyes, said to her, winking.

"No murders," Laura winked back. Even though he was sort of grotesque, she liked him. In fact, she loved him for finding this condo. "I meditate a lot, though. And do my yoga." It was so much fun to make up outlandish stories for strangers.

Her instant offer had been accepted, and the deal was already in escrow. As she looked around her Russian Hill apartment, especially at the view from the windows while sitting in the white sofa (where I've devoured so many lovely girls, she reflected, feeling her pussy tingle happily at the memory), she felt a little sad. You could see the Bay Bridge, and the fog swooping and swirling in over San Francisco Bay. The lights winked on everywhere, and you could even see Berkeley across the Bay when there was no fog. To the left was El Cerrito, where Jane and Kendra were now living. To the right was Oakland, where April lived. Where she's probably churning and groaning on top of that delicious Yolanda at this very moment, Laura thought, enviously. April's new girlfriend. Everybody needed a girlfriend.

The apartment had memories. Most of them were almost unbearably sweet. She would hate to leave it, but one had to move on. It would be such bliss to be able to relax in bed with Sara, say, in her new condo, and do whatever they liked without fear of eavesdropping. The thought of Sara brought her full circle to her obsession of the past few days, since she could not shake Sara out of her mind now, or the memory of Sara's caresses from her body either, or her funny faces, or her big soft black nipples, or her twinkling little silvery pussy ring.

And then she heard another very faint noise from upstairs and realized that Shontay was still there. And avoiding me, she thought. Since they had become lovers, Shontay would always ring Laura's buzzer whenever she came by to feed Willie, if her parents were traveling. But not tonight.

She is so jealous, Laura thought. Even just seeing me that time in the hall with Randi was enough to set her off. Think of what she must be feeling if her mother told her that the slut downstairs was having loud orgies with other women. Other black women. She wouldn't be able to let on anything, and it would kill her. She would be afraid of what her mother would think if she knew Shontay was one of those 'other women,' and she would also be filled with fury at Laura for violating their intimacy by daring to sleep with others.

This was a quandary Laura could appreciate. Understanding the depth of her own jealousies very well, she could empathize deeply with anyone who felt pangs of fierce resentment at the thought of someone else sharing the kind of physical intensity and rare ecstasy that Shontay and Laura had shared. It hurts, Laura thought. It really hurts. No wonder she feels that way.

Laura felt her own eyes glimmering with involuntary tears as she stood looking out her window, which she now knew she would be doing only a few more times. No views behind Twin Peaks, she thought. Oh, maybe a few nice trees. No city lights, though. I've got to go up there and talk to her. I've got to make her see that it doesn't make me care for her any less. I know how hurt she is. I know how she loves me to make love to her.

Sucking back her incipient tears, wiping the corners of her eyes with her wrist, she went quickly, before she could second-guess herself, snatching up her door key and sticking it into her bra for safe-keeping. In only a few more seconds, she was knocking on the Gibsons' door, remembering the last time she had done this, when Shontay had been so cold, and Laura had nearly raped her in Mr. Gibson's easy chair.

She had to stand a long time at the door, after knocking. Shontay was inside, she was sure of it, but Shontay knew, as Laura always did, that this wasn't the knock of some stranger handing out *WatchTowers*, as Jane had once suggested. She knows it has to be me. Either she's just trying to see if I'll give up and go away, or she's purposely making me squirm.

Laura knocked again, louder. Again she waited, but not as long this time. The door finally opened. Shontay did not open it only a crack, as she had done the first time.

Instead, she was bristling and hostile and opened it quite widely. She was drawn up to her full height, at least four inches taller than Laura, and her mysterious pale brown eyes, usually so mesmerizing and fascinating, glowed with anger like fierce hot embers.

"Oh . . . hi. It's me," Laura said clumsily, suddenly awkward and nervous.

"What do you want?"

"I . . ."

Laura was overcome by a hot welter of contradictory feelings. For one thing, Shontay was like two different people to her. Now, for instance, she had dropped her hair, which fell in loose clumped strands around her neck and shoulders, immeasurably softening her usual hard, imperious expression. She was enchanting like this to Laura, and physically desirable, since at work Shontay always had her hair pulled back tightly, severely, almost militarily, making her small, well-shaped head look even more regal on top of her elegant swan's neck. But she took it down when she and Laura went to bed, and that seemed to release a vulnerability in her that she never showed anywhere else, as well as a deep sensuality that Laura had exploited with careful skill.

But now . . .

She had her hair down, but the look in her eyes spelled disaster, not delicious sex. Shontay was tense with fury. It was very hard for Laura to respond to the threat as well as her own desire at the same time. God, I'm always a hopeless sucker for her when she gets this cold, aloof, imperial manner, she realized. It's her 'Off with your head!" manner. I want to drag her down on the floor and do everything to her.

"I . . . just wanted to say hello," Laura gulped.

Shontay glowered and started to close the door.

"No . . ." Laura said quickly, pushing it back open a little with the palm of one hand. "Please."

"Go away, Laura."

Laura gave Shontay her own most melting look. Shontay, I adore you, I want you, I hunger for you, for your flesh, for your wonderful long lean body, for your mouth, for your sweet little pussy, for your touch, your kiss, your low murmurs, your screams when you come. I want you. Can you see that? I want to make it up to you. I'm sorry you're hurt, but I can't help that. Let me make it better. At least for a while.

Laura shook her head.

"Then you're going to lose your fingers," Shontay snapped, trying to close the door again more forcefully.

Again, Laura had to catch it with her palm and push it back. Suddenly, they were in a struggle with the door, Shontay trying to slam it shut, Laura trying to stop her.

Laura pushed it back open with such vehemence that Shontay momentarily stumbled backward, losing her grip on the knob. Laura, in turn, stumbled forward, through the door frame, one leg into the Gibsons' apartment.

"Get out of here, you bitch!" Shontay scowled, quickly recovering her balance and grabbing Laura's elbow, trying to force her back out into the hallway.

Laura didn't budge. In fact, she pushed forward, grabbing the doorjamb for leverage. "No . . . I want to talk to you."

"You ain't got a fucking thing to say to me that I want to hear," Shontay panted, now grabbing Laura with her other hand too, trying to force her back out. "Get out of here!"

Laura relaxed and straightened up, releasing her grip on the door frame, trying to step back slowly, with dignity, giving in. It wasn't worth fighting over. She let herself be pushed back beyond the door, into the hall. She could feel the tears coming to her eyes again. Shontay's face was shockingly ugly with rage.

"I can explain," she said softly, wondering what she meant by that. What could she explain that would change Shontay's feelings?

"You can't explain shit!" Shontay spat.

"I . . . I really care about you," Laura said feebly.

"The fuck you do," Shontay hissed. "You care about black cunt, that's all."

Laura's eyes widened with indignation. "How can you say—"

"Fuck off, Laura. Go find that little teeny bopper with the braids. I'll be leaving soon. I just fed Willie. I'll be gone. You can scream and holler all you want down there. Won't be anyone here to hear you."

"Shon—"

Laura started to raise two fingers to Shontay's face, to caress her cheek, as she often did in moments of tenderness. Shontay's hand came up, and Laura was afraid she was going to knock her own hand aside. Instead, Shontay slapped her hard on the cheek, a ferocious slap, so hard that the force of it swiveled Laura's head to the side. Her palm against Laura's face made a loud crack.

Laura was so surprised that the pain did not even register for a few seconds. Stunned and hurt, she suddenly felt it flame up in her face, felt real, hot tears now spring to her eyes as she staggered slightly back, raising her fingers to her cheek. Then, to Laura's own secret horror, as if it had a life of its own, her hand lashed out and up, slapping Shontay's face equally hard, with a sharp crack too.

"Ynnnee!" Shontay yelped in shock, jumping back, dropping the doorknob, as her own head jerked to the side. She raised her fingertips to her cheek. "Oh . . . you cunt!"

Now Laura was back through the open door, into the apartment, shutting it quickly behind her as Shontay backed away further, instinctively, as if preparing for another blow. But Laura, already appalled at what she had done, had no intention of striking her again.

"Listen to me . . ." she said, trying to lower her voice, make it soothing.

"Fuck you!" Shontay swore, eyes burning, body tense, angular, and sharp, twitching with fury.

"Shontay . . . listen to me," Laura said softly, advancing.

But this time, Shontay did not give ground. She shook her head, eyes blazing red instead of pale brown now, her mouth a slash of hatred. Instead of falling back more, she advanced on Laura.

"Get out!"

Though very tall and skinny, Shontay was physically imposing merely because of her height, and she was, Laura realized, very much stronger than she looked, with a wiry, tensile force that could easily be underestimated. Without warning, she grabbed Laura's shoulders and slammed Laura back into the door.

The breath nearly left Laura's body. She could feel it being crushed out of her lungs by the impact, expelled from her throat, leaving her completely stunned and bent half over.

"Wait a . . . wait a minute," she cawed, gagging softly, gulping for breath.

"I . . . ain't . . . waiting for . . . nothing!" Shontay gasped as she grabbed Laura's arms, wrenching them, grabbing at the same time for the doorknob, slamming Laura back into the door again with a fierce frontal body block.

Of course the fact that she had Laura pinned back against the door made it hard for her to open it at the same time. Even though she was out of breath and struggling hard with Shontay, Laura realized bizarrely, that this was true, as well as the fact that Shontay, now fiercely agitated, had dropped into a kind of loose and vitriolic slang she would ordinarily avoid at all costs.

At the same time, in a split second, she was very aware of Shontay's scent, the fresh, sensual odor of her body, and her hair, which brushed Laura's cheek as Shontay shoved her violently around. Just as she had responded so sharply to Sara's fresh, unique bodily fragrance, she now found herself mesmerized by Shontay's, a scent different from Sara's but so familiar and erotic that she realized she was becoming aroused even as they were fighting.

Why am I smelling her delicious fragrance when she's trying to kill me?! Laura wondered, desperately, trying to slide to the side to avoid Shontay's angular elbows and knees.

"Get the fuck out of here, you bitch!" Shontay swore, yanking Laura forward by one wrist now so that she could get the door open.

Reaching out only to keep her balance, Laura's fingers caught in the collar of Shontay's shirt, and as Shontay elbowed her roughly to the side, the fabric ripped and the buttons popped off all in one motion. Laura was left with a handful of cloth, still half-attached to Shontay's body, buttons clattering as they hit the floor.

Shontay's delicious, smooth, light brown skin was visible through the jagged rips in her shirt, and the shiny violet sateen fabric of her bra also showed. She looked down at her torn shirt in disbelief.

"Oh god, you little shit, Laura, it's my favorite blouse!" she screamed, lashing out with her hand again, the back of it this time, her knuckles catching Laura along the jaw, not a direct impact but enough to send her to her knees.

This time, Laura was a little dizzy, but she somehow felt, looking up into Shontay's blazing eyes, that Shontay too was feeling the strange, potent mixture of anger and sexual excitement that Laura was feeling. And she could also see in Shontay's eyes that she too felt it and knew Laura recognized it, and that she was implacably determined not to let it go any farther.

Shontay stumbled and lurched toward the door again, reaching for the knob, but Laura now, really for the first time, grabbed her, wrapping both arms around one of Shontay's legs to keep her from moving. Shontay was wearing pants, but Laura could feel the coiled strength of her leg under the cloth, flexing and straining, as she held on, pulling Shontay back, whimpering and trying to reason with her at the same time.

"Listen to me . . . damn you!" she hissed, barely able to speak from shortness of breath. "I want to . . . apologize."

"Fuck you!" Shontay swore, her lovely face grimacing in hatred. "Get out of here! I'm going to call the cops! Get out of here . . . you don't have my permission to be here . . . you're breaking and entering! You despicable slut, you whore, you fucking dyke! I hate you!"

Laura was desolated by these accusations. Feeling defeated and sickened, she relaxed her grip on Shontay's leg, almost ready to give in completely and leave. But Shontay was still so stiff with rage that she again stumbled, reaching for the doorknob, and her leg still entangled in Laura's arms, she fell to the floor beside Laura, an awkward heap of limbs and knobby elbows and knees, squealing a little with surprise as she fell.

"Ynnneeeee! Oh!" she yelped, twisting to free her leg from Laura's grasp. "Let me go, you cunt!"

Laura clenched her teeth, glaring at Shontay. "Quit calling me those names!"

"Fuck you!"

Eyes blazing, Shontay again lashed out with her hand, smacking Laura hard against the side of the head, aiming for her cheek but missing. Instinctively, Laura leaned forward, extending both arms, reaching with her hands for Shontay's long, exquisite neck. She had never choked anyone in her life, but something in her drove her to do it at this instant. She grabbed Shontay's neck with both hands, pushing her back, lunging over her, not really wanting to strangle or kill her but to threaten her seriously enough to make her stop.

Shontay's hands flailed at her back, pounding Laura, pummeling her wildly.

"Ungghh! Let me go! You . . . you fucking . . . you—"

But now Laura's own retaliatory fury was in gear, and she could feel a hot, sharp energy of defensive anger flood her own body. Continuing to push Shontay down, down onto her back, her fingers closed around the girl's long, beautiful neck. She did not close them tightly, though. The feel of Shontay's smooth, warm skin under her fingers was a much too sensual drug. She had kissed this beautiful swan's neck so often, and whimpered into it when coming deliriously in Shontay's arms.

"Oh god . . . you are such a cunt!" Shontay panted, struggling under Laura, rolling and pitching back and forth, trying to throw Laura off.

Her hands found their way under Laura's sweatshirt, and she clawed Laura's back, chuffing and gasping and churning desperately. God, it's almost like we were fucking, Laura realized.

"Ouchhhh! Laura yelped, tightening her fingers now on Shontay's lovely throat to make her stop. "Don't do that. Don't hurt me."

"Fuck you!" Shontay glowered up at her. "Didn't you hear me? Fuck you! FUCK YOU!"

But even though she was digging and clawing at Laura's naked back, she was not doing it the way Randi or Sholandra had once done. Her fingernails were not breaking Laura's skin. Maybe she thinks I'm going to strangle her, Laura thought. Or maybe she's feeling something like I am, like this is almost like fucking.

Laura loosened her grip, melting. I want her. Oh god, I never wanted her as much as this! I wonder if she feels that way too. She realized that her own pussy was burbling and flooding with juice. The wetness in her crotch was amazing. I wonder if she . . .

They were still tussling and struggling and panting on the floor, and Laura purposely let Shontay roll her to the side, off her body, so that she could maneuver one hand down in the vicinity of her thighs. Even though Shontay was wearing jeans, she was evidently creaming so much that the damp dew on the denim over her crotch was unmistakable as Laura's fingertips grazed it.

It was really all Laura needed to know. She had found it hard to keep her mouth off Shontay's alluring, exposed, light caramel skin up until now, and now she gave in to the impulse, leaning closer, mashing her lips aggressively into Shontay's bare shoulder, just above her shoulder blade, through a gap in her torn shirt. Laura ran her lips hungrily all over it, then across another torn strip of fabric up to Shontay's long neck, kissing it too passionately.

"Ohhnnnn!" Shontay cried out in her fury. "Ummmmggghh!"

Laura could feel her body quiver, though whether it was from sexual arousal or fresh rage she couldn't tell. But it didn't take long to find out.

"Arrngghhhh!" Shontay grunted loudly, flinging Laura off her body with almost supernatural strength, extending her arms and violently pushing Laura away. "Let go of me, you cunt! You dyke, you fucking perverted dyke! Let go of me! God, I hate you! I hate you!"

But, knowing that Shontay was aroused too, Laura was not about to give in now. True, Shontay had swelled up with a new hot bubble of fury, her pale brown eyes fiery and flaming with ferocity, her body—wildly desirable to Laura now that her shirt hung in tatters around her smooth, exposed flesh, her hair mussed and askew—stiff and tense with anger.

"I want you," Laura said, very softly, her eyes pleading. "I'm sorry. I want you."

"I hate you!" Shontay screamed. "I don't ever want you to touch me again!"

Laura knew that if she didn't overpower her, there was a lot of danger waiting for her in those long, flailing arms and legs. With a swift, gliding move, she leaned forward and again pushed Shontay onto her back, sliding one of her own thighs between Shontay's, and pulling off the shredded blouse as much as she could, pressing her lips to Shontay's half-naked body everywhere she could.

She brought her thigh up quickly and pushed it into Shontay's crotch, writhing with her, groping, sucking her long, exquisite neck.

"Oh! Oh!" Shontay whimpered, trying to free herself, but not half as hard as she had tried earlier.

Laura was wearing a sweatshirt, which was hard to tear or rip off, but Shontay's scrabbling fingers tore at it anyway, now pulling it up. Her hands raced frantically over Laura's bare skin, as if she could not make up her mind whether to scratch or caress Laura. Her quick, darting fingers pulled up the cups from Laura's bra, freeing Laura's breasts. She grabbed and twisted Laura's nipples sharply.

"Aiieeee!" Laura cried out, feeling stabbing flames shoot through her nipples and her breasts.

It was a violent attack, but it was, she knew, also very close to what they might do together sexually. She and Shontay had never indulged in the semi-rough sex that Laura had frequently experienced with some others, but what was this moment if not a sexual collision of the most acute kind?

"Oh shit . . . that hurts!" Laura glowered at her, eyes watering. "Get off me, you cunt!"

Laura slapped her. Up until now she had not struck back except in self-defense, but this time her hand flew up automatically, cracking Shontay alongside the jaw. Shontay was still lying half under her, and she was so stunned by the slap that Laura tore the remnants of her blouse away with little trouble, ripping it up, grabbing Shontay's bare shoulders, her frenzied fingers pulling and tearing at Shontay's bra straps at the same time.

Shontay's eyes, already hot with anger, suddenly flared with a thermonuclear fire that Laura had not seen there before. Reaching up with both long arms, she grabbed thick fistfuls of Laura's hair in both hands and yanked it hard. Laura's scalp exploded in pain, but it was a pain of a different quality than Shontay had probably intended. It hurt like hell, but since her experiences with Dawn and Deshona, it also was a sexual turn-on of colossal dimensions, and Laura could feel her whole body suddenly run with flame, her pussy throbbing wildly.

"Annniieeeee!" she heard herself shrieking and squealing. "Oh god . . . you bitch . . . Shontay, you bitch, let go!"

Her eyes were blurred with pain as the two of them now rolled and thrashed around on the floor as Laura tried to loosen Shontay's grip on her hair, but she could now get her hands on Shontay's beautiful violet-colored bra without obstruction. It was a pity to destroy underwear so beautiful, but without remorse, Laura tore it from Shontay's body with two violent jerks. The snaps in the back popped, and the bra simply crumpled in her hands.

"Oh shit . . ." Shontay gasped, looking down as her small, naked, teacup-shaped breasts and glimmering dark caramel nipples came into view, swaying and jiggling as she struggled with Laura.

Shontay was still yanking Laura's hair, but Laura was all over Shontay's naked upper body in a flash, squeezing her small breasts, pinching her nipples, though not as sharply as Shontay had pinched hers, then sucking them voraciously, hungrily, yelping at first as Shontay took a few more hard pulls of her hair, then groaning softly and sucking hard.

"Oh! Oh!" Shontay gulped, quickly overcome by Laura's fierce passion, her fingers relaxing, releasing the clumps of Laura's hair she had been pulling. "Ohhhnnnnn . . . oh god!"

This brief second of relaxation on Shontay's part gave Laura the chance to unfasten the zipper of the girl's jeans, while she was still hungrily sucking and mouth-mauling Shontay's nipples, and in the midst of doing it she realized that Shontay was really not resisting any longer. She even lifted her butt a little as Laura pulled the jeans over her hips and down her legs, now slipping lower, kissing her heaving stomach, running her lips all over the smooth, quivering muscles and lovely warm light brown skin.

Shontay's hands were plucking spastically at the shoulders of Laura's sweatshirt, pulling it up, as if she were trying to get it off too, and Laura quickly obliged her by hurriedly lifting it over her head and throwing it across the small entryway. As she hurriedly unfastened her scrunched-up bra, which Shontay had roughly pulled up to expose her breasts, she heard the door key she had hidden there clatter against the hardwood floor as it fell. Quickly Shontay's own fingers ran feverishly over Laura's skin too, digging into Laura's flesh.

Laura slid up again, sucking her neck, kissing her ear, her cheek, her jaw, gently pinching Shontay's saliva-wet nipples.

"I want you," she breathed.

"Fuck you," Shontay glowered at her, turning her head. "Don't you touch me."

"What if I do?"

"I'll kill you." Shontay slid the fingers of both hands into Laura's hair again as a threat.

"I'll fuck you."

"I'll kill you. You cunt."

She bucked her body, trying to throw Laura off, pulling Laura's hair again too, but not as roughly as before. Laura was very preoccupied in struggling out of her own jeans, and her panties, but she cried out as the fiery pain in her scalp flared yet again.

"Ohhnnnggaaiiieeee! Oh shit! Don't you ever stop? Owwwwwcchhh! That hurts!"

"Get off me . . . you cunt."

By now they were both completely naked, except for Shontay's panties, pale violet beauties that matched the bra Laura had destroyed. Laura slid her hands down the girl's long, smooth body to them, but immediately Shontay tightened her grip on Laura's hair, actually yanking Laura's head up so that Laura was face to face with her.

"Don't you touch me," she warned.

Looking directly into her eyes, Laura slid her fingers under the elastic band, down to one of Shontay's gorgeous tight little hard round buns. She cradled it in her palm, squeezing it gently. She could even feel a little warm cunt juice from Shontay's inflamed quim dripping down onto this delightful ripe globe of flesh, which moistened her fingers.

Oh god, she wants it as much as I do! Laura realized.

She leaned forward again, mashing the entire length of her naked body into Shontay's, noticing that she had left a little mark on Shontay's long, spectacular neck earlier, sucking it again in the same spot, sucking harder this time, so that Shontay began to squirm again under her, and again relaxed her fingers in Laura's hair.

"Unhhh! Don't do that! Unhhh! Laura . . . stop . . ."

"You . . . want it," Laura panted. "Just like . . . me."

"No," Shontay gasped, now panting too, still struggling under Laura, but writhing excitedly more than trying to escape. "No . . . don't touch me . . . ohhhhhh!"

Laura breathed a hot stream of air into her ear. At the same time, she pulled Shontay's panties down, down, down her thighs, down to her knees, which required her momentarily to slide further down the girl's long body. Shontay's long, scissoring legs were like the blades of some deadly piece of machinery, kicking and jerking at intervals up into the air.

Laura slid down, pinning the girl's thrashing legs under her, and forcibly tore Shontay's panties down and off her feet. Oh god, I want to eat her pussy, she realized, suddenly inhaling the hot, pungent odors of Shontay's aroused slit, but she knew it was too risky, since Shontay was still seething with anger. Instead, Laura slid back up, embracing her, pinning her to the floor, but dropping one hand again to Shontay's thighs, dipping it between them.

"Laura, don't you touch me!" Shontay whimpered, suddenly letting her torso fall back to the floor, her fingers now running in a frenzy over Laura's bare shoulders, then digging into Laura's back. "Don't you touch me! No!"

Laura slid two fingers up into the soupy crease of Shontay's sweet, small pussy almost before Shontay knew what was happening.

"Ahhnngggg!" Shontay gagged softly, arching her back slightly so that her small, lovely breasts bobbed in circles.

Even though they had shared some hot sex, Laura knew Shontay had never been this wet before. Not with me, at least. God, she's flooding, Laura thought. Her fingers were slathered with warm slippery fluids as she twisted them inside the tight, warm, very wet channel. Gee, I could fist fuck her, Laura thought, but knew she had better not. It was bad enough that they had struggled so hard to get to this point without adding a fresh perversity to shock and repel Shontay further.

But she didn't mind taunting her a little.

"You want me to fuck you," she chanted softly, beginning to move her hand, to rub one knuckle up against Shontay's clit, to apply clever pressure that would increase Shontay's need.

"No," Shontay gasped, shaking her head vigorously, frowning.

"You want to fuck me too," Laura chanted, feeling a very strong fluttering and hot pulsing in her own cunt, wanting desperately for Shontay to touch it too, so they could both dissolve into a molten frenzy of fucking she knew they each needed terribly.

She felt Shontay's fingernails against the bare flesh of her thigh and for a second wondered if Shontay were going to scratch her. But then she opened her thighs a little, rolling sideways partially off Shontay's body, so that Shontay could get her hand into the right position. And then . . .

She felt one of Shontay's long, thin fingers slip between her pussy lips, then slide up inside.

"Oh god . . . yes! Unhhhhh! Oh yes, honey . . . fuck me too, yes!"

But Shontay, even though she now had her finger in Laura's pussy too, refused to acknowledge in her facial expression that anything had changed. Her pale, mysterious brown eyes throbbed, though, seeming to reflect a deeper sexual trance, but she continued to shake her head slowly from side to side. Laura believed it was now okay to kiss her, and she did so without any warning, not wanting to give Shontay a chance to turn her head away or otherwise repulse her.

She leaned forward quickly and caught Shontay's mouth with her own, kissing her savagely, forcing her tongue between Shontay's sensual lips and now sliding her fingers up the girl's clit, rubbing it in tight, rapid swirls in exactly the way she had seen Shontay do herself when masturbating. It was a scorching, direct assault. With her free hand, Laura reached down again and cupped one of Shontay's small, firm buns, digging her fingertips into the warm, smooth, spongy flesh.

"Oh!" Shontay whimpered. "Oh . . . Laura!" she murmured against Laura's devouring mouth.

Laura did not let her speak. Again, she forced her tongue deep into Shontay's mouth, now gyrating her own hips so that Shontay's hand had to move in her own crotch, whether Shontay wanted to move it or not. Now, Laura exulted, they were fucking. You couldn't call it anything else, and she could feel Shontay's body beginning to undulate and squirm in spite of herself.

Laura rolled on top of her again and began to screw her in earnest now, dropping her mouth to Shontay's dark caramel nipples, her lips tearing at them, her hand plunging, swirling, rubbing, as she heard Shontay's whimpers growing more desperate and felt her body straining and churning. This moment of snuffling and soft groaning and squirming, rubbing their naked bodies together, seemed to be suspended in time for Laura, who wanted it never to end and allowed herself to experience each infinitesimal twinge and pulse of her own body and Shontay's, luxuriating in the feel of Shontay's silky wet pussy flesh against her probing fingers, loving the soft chewy sensation of Shontay's stiffening nipples against her tongue.

"Oh yes . . . honey . . . oh yes, honey," Laura purred, panting, sucking, again running her free hand up Shontay's body to her face, interlacing her fingers now in Shontay's hair, even pulling it slightly, not hard, but almost a reminder of the way she had pulled Laura's.

Shontay, though her eyes were pulsing and throbbing in the slow whirl of a gathering sexual storm, focused them on Laura for a second and lifted her hand too, sliding her long thin fingers again into Laura's hair.

"Yes . . ." Laura murmured, wildly excited, suddenly feeling a few preliminary twinges of her own coming orgasm in her pussy, which

Shontay was now rubbing and fucking more deliberately. "Yes . . . pull my hair," she glowered at Shontay, a threat, a plea, a promise.

Shontay bit her lower lip, panting, her eyelids fluttering, her pelvis swirling and bucking under Laura's body. "I . . . hate you," she gulped, glaring at Laura, then groaning softly as her eyes rolled up. "I hate you . . . Laura . . . unngghhh! Oh god!"

"Yes!"

"Unh! Unh!"

Shontay almost lost control, but then quickly recovered, tightening her grip on her fistfuls of Laura's hair. With two fingers sunk in the girl's warm, buttery slit, her palm facing Shontay's pubic bone, Laura scissored Shontay's clitoral hood between her forefinger and middle finger and began to rub up and down, forcibly, passionately, sucking her neck again, and softly whinnying as her own climax began to overwhelm her.

"Oh Shontay!"

"Ungghh! I . . . hate you! Ungghhh!"

Laura began to come and yanked Shontay's hair in her hand, sharply, for the first time. She knew Shontay would come any second too, and this would probably tip her over the edge. She could see the fires leap up in Shontay's shocked eyes as the pain hit her. Then Laura could feel Shontay's grip tightening even further.

"Auungghgghh!" Laura cried out in a wild shriek of mingled pain and sexual exuberance as she felt Shontay pull her hair in a violent yank.

A surging, roiling orgasm wrenched her body, but through it she could hear Shontay's ecstatic groaning and feel her gyrating hips almost rising off the floor, shuddering, bucking, as Shontay too erupted in a thrilling climax right behind her.

"Ohhnnmmmgggiiieee!" Shontay squealed, writhing in a fierce seizure of ecstasy under Laura, her hands both pulling Laura's hair still with amazing strength, sparking to life new hot jolts of coming in Laura's throbbing pussy.

Laura, on the other hand, released Shontay's hair at this moment, letting her hand fall to the girl's lovely bare shoulders instead, then caressing her neck, where, even in her stunned and throbbing condition, she noticed the dark, speckled blood blotch she had raised on the smooth, light brown column of beautiful flesh. Oh god, now she'll hate me even more, she thought, hearing Shontay's labored breathing in her ear, feeling Shontay's long, lithe body begin to relax as the last twitches of her orgasm died away.

Finally, Shontay too released Laura's hair, which now fell in a large, shiny flag over her face as Laura slowly drew her body up to look in Shontay's eyes. She tossed her head to get it out of their way, relishing the glow that was now clearly visible in Shontay's pale, burning eyes, the unmistakable lingering heat of a stupendous sexual explosion. Shontay might still hate her, but she would remember this fuck for a long time.

"Still hate me?" Laura whispered, daring her to lie.

Shontay could not suppress a small, involuntary grin as it crossed her delicious, sensual lips, which Laura felt like assaulting again, this instant.

"Yes."

"Even after that?"

"I didn't want it."

"You loved it."

The sly, helpless little grin again. "I . . . couldn't help it."

Slowly, Laura rolled to the side, feeling she might be too heavy since she had been lying on top of Shontay for quite a while now. Shontay actually grabbed her hips and her lower back to keep her from moving.

"No . . . stay there."

"Really?"

Shontay nodded slowly, solemnly. "I like the way it feels with you on top of me."

"In that case, I will never move."

Laura kissed her. This time, Shontay, as if she were a different person, yielded completely to Laura's mouth, and her tongue, raising her hands and lightly caressing Laura's naked back through a long, expressive, emotional kiss. When it was over, she gazed dreamily up into Laura's eyes, trailing one forefinger along Laura's cheek.

"I guess this is the second time you raped me, right?"

Laura gave her a long face. "How could you say such a thing? I couldn't help myself either." She lowered her voice to a sexy growl. "Because I know how hot you are. You make my blood sizzle."

"You are such a fucking liar, Laura."

Laura plunged boldly forward. "I only came up here to ask you down to dinner."

Shontay cocked one eyebrow, maliciously. "What are you serving, black cunt? It's all you like to eat, isn't it?"

Again, Laura moved to get off Shontay's body, but Shontay again held her hips to keep her there. Her eyes, so light brown and mysterious and lovely, bored up into Laura's.

"Don't move. It still feels good."

"You insulted me," Laura pouted.

Shontay's eyes became suddenly dreamy again. "You pulled my hair. God, I came hard. I never knew that would happen."

Laura leaned forward and kissed the blood bruise she had raised on Shontay's lovely neck, which Shontay, of course, did not yet know was there. "If you come downstairs with me," Laura murmured, "I can guarantee one of us is going to eat some black cunt at least."

Shontay broke into a smile. "Now you know why I tried to keep you out. Once I let you in, it's just rape rape rape."

Laura smiled back. "And fuck fuck fuck. Right?"

"I never knew I was this kind of person."

"And what `kind of person' would that be?"

"I don't know . . . sex fiend?"

"Can I take that as an answer to my invitation?"

Shontay sat up and Laura obligingly rolled off her. Laura kissed her shoulder.

"Help me clean Willie's litter box, and I'll come down there with you," Shontay whispered. "We probably scared the living shit out of him with all this fighting and screaming." She looked around them in amazement. "On the floor, too. God . . ."

Shontay was right. Laura had not seen Willie the whole time. Apparently, he had high-tailed it for safety when these two screeching harpies had attacked each other and ended up on the floor fucking like two wild animals. Enough to scare the wits out of any calm, domestic feline. Laura was a little sad about it. She liked Willie, and he had always liked her.

Laura inched closer, embracing her so that their upper bodies, still deliciously naked, pressed together. "Are you sorry?"

Shontay shook her head. "I guess not. You are a liar and a bitch, though. Don't think I don't see through you."

"Did you know you're wildly sexy when you're angry?" Laura said, to deflect her bitterness, which was still apparent.

"Quit trying to change the subject," Shontay said, getting to her feet. "And quit staring at me. I feel like an awkward little girl at the doctor's, or something."

She helped Laura up with one hand, but Laura could not take her eyes off Shontay's tall, thin, but still supple and desirable naked body. Shontay's small, swaying breasts were enchanting, her nipples dark caramel-colored and shiny, tongue-tempting.

As she rose to her feet, Laura held onto Shontay's hand for a moment, drawing her close. "I love your body," she said seriously. "I love it. I want it."

They stood staring deeply into each other's eyes for a few seconds, silent, holding each other's gaze. Then Shontay bent to retrieve her clothes, even the ripped up blouse.

"The litter's in the kitchen, under the sink," she said. "Bring it back to the bathroom and I'll empty the box."

In her absence, Laura searched the hardwood floor for her door key, which she found hidden behind an umbrella stand, then quickly slipped back into her clothes before going to fetch the litter.

In Laura's apartment, Shontay was again stiff and withdrawn. I can't believe she's still angry with me after that glorious fuck upstairs, Laura thought. But then she relented. She had no idea what Shontay's mother—surely it had been her mother; not that dignified old cluck of a father, surely he wouldn't dare bring it up—had told her. Mrs. Gibson might have made it pretty lurid.

Since Laura had ripped apart her favorite blouse, and her bra too, Shontay had found one of her mother's housecoats in the closet and put it on before going with Laura down to Laura's apartment. The housecoat—more a kimono, really, of yellow silk with a pattern of large flamingo-colored flowers on it—made Shontay look both a little dowdy and wildly fetching at the same time. How that could be, Laura didn't know, but just watching her move around with this thin silk thing veiling her long, angular, bony body made Laura wet and hungry for her all over again.

The yellow of the silk was especially alluring against the smooth dark-honey glow of Shontay's marvelous skin.

"I lied," Laura said to her as she fastened the door locks. "I really wasn't fixing dinner. I just wanted to get you down here."

Again the faint, sly little grin that had passed over Shontay's lips earlier returned. "See, I told you you were a fucking liar," she said without, however, smiling more broadly.

Laura stepped closer, lowering her voice, and her eyelids. "I want to take off this kimono thing and kiss you everywhere," she breathed.

Shontay remained coy. "I kind of liked it when you ripped my clothes off. It made me realize you really wanted me."

Laura ran a fingertip across the silk collar of the kimono, then let it slip over the edge onto Shontay's skin. Then she slipped the finger under the silk.

"We shouldn't harm your mother's kimono. She might get suspicious."

But she realized that Shontay was not looking at her but over her shoulder. There was a long oval hallway mirror next to Laura's door, which she often used for a brief check before dashing out. Shontay was squinting into the mirror, her face suddenly reflecting her horror as she raised her hand to her neck, which Laura was about to kiss again, for the umpteenth time.

For a second, Laura thought Shontay was going to strike her again, with the back of her hand. Her face, when screwed up like this in sudden anger, was ferocious and completely scary, as if a mad, slashing fury were about to pour forth.

"Oh god . . . you gave me a hickey!" Shontay wailed, her voice keening upward as she touched the bruise on her beautiful neck with two fingertips, gingerly.

She almost shoved Laura out of the way in her haste to get closer to the mirror. She examined it with intense interest.

"I . . . didn't mean to," Laura stammered awkwardly.

Now Shontay was leaning even closer to the mirror, framing a large portion of her exquisite long neck with the fingers of both hands, tilting her head to the side. Laura found her neck breath-taking anyway and had in truth given her the hickey in a wild, irresistible paroxysm of scorching lust. Looking at it, as Shontay exposed the beautiful expanse of skin to the mirror so she could get a closer look herself, Laura was almost overcome by a fresh wave of the same lust. Somehow, the uneven, purplish blotch on Shontay's perfect light brown skin was exquisitely erotic to her.

She put a hand on Shontay's shoulder, half afraid it would be shrugged off violently. But they had apparently moved beyond the fighting stage, and Shontay was not tense as she turned her face to Laura. All the quick fury had drained out of it, and she was soft and sexy, her eyes alluring, flashing with invitations.

"Nobody ever gave me a hickey before," she said in a hushed voice. "Not that I like it, you cunt. How am I going to cover this up?"

"Mmmm, I could kiss it . . . maybe it'll go away," Laura purred, lifting one swatch of Shontay's hair and nibbling her earlobe.

Shontay giggled, finding this ticklish. "You'll only make it worse."

Laura's lips reached her neck, but she veered away from the hickey, still lifting Shontay's hair, kissing the back of her neck, pulling down the kimono a little to kiss the nape of her neck.

"I could give you a matching one on the other side," she teased.

Shontay shivered, a sharp tremor. "God, you're getting me all excited again."

"Oh good. Come with me." Laura took her hand. "Or did you want me to fix dinner first?"

Shontay smiled, for the first time a warm, girlish, happy, sexual smile. "No. Later."

In Laura's bed, this time there was no struggle, no anger, just slow and devastatingly thorough sensuality. Laura was surprised by the transformation that came over Shontay, who seemed to have received a fresh charge of nasty lechery by the realization that Laura had, unbeknownst to her until now, given her a hickey while fighting and fucking with her on the floor upstairs. She swarmed over Laura, never giving Laura a chance to get the upper hand, which was usual for them, since Shontay was usually the receiver more than the giver.

"Let me, you know, do you in the ass . . . like you do me once in a while," she breathed hotly in Laura's ear. "You always get to have all the fun. Let me stick my finger up your ass and make you scream."

This was enough to make flames leap up happily inside Laura's body. "Are you sure you want to?" Never in the past had Shontay showed any desire to be 'creative.'

Shontay was kissing Laura's neck passionately and replied only by nipping Laura's earlobe. "You are such a bitch . . . I want to make you scream," she murmured sexily. "I want to give you a hickey too."

"Oh god . . . I think you're doing it!" Laura squirmed, feeling hot fire squirt through her pussy as Shontay sucked her neck. "Here . . . honey . . . unhhhhh! Oh! God, that feels good! Here, I'll get the oil for you."

Shontay moderated her love attack long enough for Laura to lean across the bed to the bedside table and open the drawer. She handed the small bottle of baby oil to Shontay, and their eyes locked, throbbing, expectant.

"Do you want a towel?"

Shontay shook her head, her eyes not releasing Laura's. Her stiffish, mussed hair swished around her ears and her neck, making her wildly sexy to Laura. I would let her do anything to me right now, Laura thought. She's so . . . intense. I think she's still really angry at me, but she is full of fuck hunger right now.

For all her usual reserve, Shontay was at the moment apparently overcome by sheer sexual need. Laura was right. As she lay back, Shontay was suddenly all over her again, kissing and stroking her body more aggressively than she had ever done, sucking Laura's nipples hungrily for the first time that night. Still clutching the small plastic bottle, which Laura could feel against her bare skin as Shontay moved over her squirming body, kissing and stroking and sucking it as she descended toward Laura's groin, she finally slid down between Laura's yawning thighs.

"Oh!" Laura gasped as she felt Shontay's lips against her pussy for the first time in weeks.

In keeping with her present mood, Shontay did not waste her time on tenderness or subtlety. Whether it was her desire for Laura or her residual anger from the fight they had had upstairs, she was rough and hungry, spreading Laura's cunt lips with her thumbs and slurping Laura's hot, achy slit passionately. Laura, though hotly aroused, had come quickly and explosively upstairs and was in little danger of coming again too quickly.

Instead, during the next few minutes, she enjoyed and endured a flurry of passion from Shontay that was as startling as it was thrilling. Shontay licked and fingered her cunt rapidly, hungrily, sucking Laura's clit, sliding her fingers between Laura's buns, doing everything to Laura that she had felt Laura do to her in the past. Laura nearly fainted with pleasure, writhing, panting, whimpering as she felt Shontay turn up the heat even further.

"Mmmm, you like that, don't you, you nasty white girl," Shontay grinned up at her, twisting her fingers inside of Laura's pussy, making Laura groan with sexual excitement.

"Unngghhhh! Oh! Aunngghh! Yes . . . yes, honey, do it! Oh Jesus, that feels good!"

"You want me to fuck your little white ass, don't you?" Shontay panted, eyes flaring.

It was so bizarre, Laura realized in the back of her mind. Of all her lovers, Shontay was among the most sophisticated and reserved: regal, college-educated, two professors for parents, in upper management herself, refined, self-controlled, well-mannered. Yet in her lust and anger, she had degenerated into these flagrant racial taunts and insults, which somehow pleased her. She's getting back at me for hurting her, Laura realized. And Laura was a little intimidated by it, but at the same time loved the fierceness that Shontay was showing. They had never had any rough sex together until this evening, but Laura was quickly becoming aware that it wasn't over yet.

There was a brief pause in the onslaught while Shontay fumbled with the snap-open top of the bottle. Laura, lying flat on her back with her thighs spread, feeling ready to be roughly ravished by this fierce beautiful girl who had no idea of her own stark, almost aristocratic appeal, watched in fascination as Shontay spread baby oil all over one long, thin finger. In the middle of lubricating her finger, Shontay's eyes flashed at her.

"You want it?"

Laura nodded. "I want you to do everything to me."

Shontay smiled ambiguously and snapped shut the bottle, leaning across Laura to place it on the bed stand, her small, exquisite breasts swaying delightfully. Laura reached up to touch them, gently scissoring Shontay's nipples in her fingers.

"Let me suck you."

"No." Shontay shook her head, frowning. "I've got something I'm doing."

"Do you know how beautiful you are?"

Shontay grinned. "Quit trying to change the subject."

With a raised eyebrow, she slithered down between Laura's thighs again. Laura felt Shontay's other hand pulling open her ass cheeks, then felt Shontay's greasy fingertip press against her asshole, then felt the long digit slide up into her so deep that it felt twice as long as she knew it was.

"Unnhhh!" she gasped, water coming to her eyes. "Oh . . . yes!"

Shontay grinned up at her, twisting her finger, watching Laura's face. "You like that?"

"Oh yes!"

"How do you like this?"

She began to fuck Laura's asshole very fast with her finger, plunging it in deep, giving Laura short rabbit jabs with it, biting her lower lip in concentration at the same time. Laura was slightly afraid of the glint in Shontay's pale brown eyes, but she was also very aroused by this sharp, thrusting attack. And now Shontay bent her mouth to Laura's pussy too, tonguing and sucking the inflamed cunt lips, taking Laura's throbbing clit into her mouth as her long finger continued to pierce Laura's anus in quick jabs.

"Oh god . . . oh god!" Laura heard herself whimpering, twisting her body, looking down at the maniacal smile on Shontay's face, feeling the sweet pressure of a sexual storm begin to swell in her flesh.

Oh god, I think I might come sooner than I thought, she realized, feeling overwhelmed by Shontay's aggressive hunger. Shontay was fucking her furiously, but the fury and passion seemed to grow out of a confused mixture of desire for Laura's body and hot anger at her at the same time. Then, completely unexpectedly, Shontay, still leaving her finger buried in Laura's clenching ass, slid up to kiss her.

Her torso and her arms were so long that she could do this with relative ease, and as they coiled their tongues together, panting and mewling, she kept fucking Laura's ass slowly and relentlessly with her finger. At the same time, she rubbed her forearm above the wrist into the sopping-wet crease of Laura's swollen pussy, pushing it hard into Laura's splayed cunt, mashing it against Laura's clit, then furiously jabbing Laura's asshole again with her long finger.

"Unhhh! Ohnnn! Ungghhh!" Laura grunted softly, her eyes rolling up, nearly losing it until she felt Shontay's mouth again on her own, tearing savagely at her lips, Shontay's strong, probing tongue nearly sliding down her throat. "Oh shit! Unh! Yes! Oh god . . . Shontay . . . ungghhh!"

"You are such a bitch!" Shontay hissed into Laura's teeth, but without the slightest sign of anger on her face. "I want you to come so hard. So hard . . . like you make me come. I want you to just die when you come."

"I . . . think you're going to get your wish," Laura gasped, now undulating, pushing her ass down into the upward thrusts of Shontay's hand, feeling her flesh pulse and throb with the first hints of an arriving orgasm.

Shontay was a whirlwind. Laura had never seen her like this, a hot tornado, cradling Laura's shoulders in her arms and fucking Laura's ass furiously with her other hand, mashing her forearm into Laura's pussy, kissing and sucking Laura's neck, then dropping her mouth to Laura's breasts, tearing at her nipples, before moving her head up again to see the contortions of intense pleasure and near-desperation on Laura's face.

Laura's hands fluttered up spasmodically, trying to clutch Shontay's body, trying to caress her and embrace her, but she was quickly overcome by the intensity and sharp passion of Shontay's fuck-assault. She could feel her fingertips brush Shontay's erect nipples, even feel the firm, smooth flesh of her small breasts, and the ripple of her ribcage, the wave-like up and down motion of her hard stomach as she breathed rapidly. But she could not get a grip on the girl's squirming body anywhere, and soon her own body was engulfed by spasms so acute that it became pointless anyway.

"Auungghhh!" Laura cried out, her body suddenly arching of its own accord into the air, almost levitating off the mattress.

As Laura collapsed back to the bed, Shontay gave her a crushing embrace, so fierce that she wondered where the girl's strength had come from. Shontay was now half on top of her, still fucking her furiously, and whimpering and gasping too with incredible sexual excitement. Laura felt a pulverizing bolt of hot coming rip through her, nearly knocking her breath out.

"Unngghhh!"

"Oh yes . . . oh Laura yes!" Shontay gasped, as her hand stopped thrusting and she held Laura in a death grip.

"Auungghh!" Laura finally cried out again as her breath returned. "Mnnngghiiieeeee! Ohnnnnggg! Mnnngghiiieeeee!"

A ferocious climax wrenched her. She shuddered violently, undulating in long, involuntary waves as a stream of wracking spasms poured through her shaking body. For a brief few seconds, she became unaware of anything else, unaware of Shontay holding her, of Shontay's finger thrust up her ass, of Shontay's hard, bony forearm mashed into her throbbing cunt. Only the white-hot wrenching spasms of her orgasm filled her consciousness, until they began to grow less strong, less frequent, and she drifted back to awareness to find herself still in Shontay's death grip.

After a few seconds, even though Laura was thrilled to be held so tightly, it began to hurt.

"Could you . . . let me go for a minute?" she panted, looking up almost worshipfully into Shontay's warm, pale brown eyes, now soft with sexual caring. "I . . . can't breathe."

Shontay smiled and released her grip. "Sorry. I got carried away. I never made you, or anybody, come like that."

"Not me, at least," Laura gulped, slowly rubbing her arms where Shontay had clasped them so fiercely.

Now Shontay was totally serious and concerned, her solicitude so far removed from her earlier sexual rage and mania that at first Laura had trouble getting used to it.

Shontay, in contrast to being stiff with anger and spite, was soft and pliant, warm and affectionate, stroking Laura's shoulder, cupping Laura's breast, her lips parted and inviting. Laura leaned up and kissed her, at the same time looping one arm behind Shontay's neck and drawing her down to the bed again.

They kissed very sweetly for about a minute, Laura's hand crawling up to Shontay's small, wonderful breasts and squeezing them suggestively.

"I hope you know you aren't getting away with that," she whispered when their lips came apart.

Shontay grinned, almost bashfully. "You mean you're going to pay me back?"

"What do you think?" Laura said, rolling her onto her back. "I'm going to give you a matching hickey on the other side."

Shontay suddenly winced in fear. "Oh . . . please don't! One is enough. God, I'll have to hide it with makeup or something."

Laura snuggled up to her, kissing her under the chin, nipping her ear. "If I don't, will you let me lick that beautiful little pussy of yours? I've been dying to all night."

Shontay nodded. "I will . . . let you."

Laura smiled and kissed her cheek, then her neck again, right on the plum-colored splotch of the hickey she had given her. "I promise to make it up to you for this," she whispered.

Laura loved Shontay's body. Though it was long and thin, a little bony and angular in places, you would never know that under her clothes, Shontay had this high, round, pert little ass, so beautifully hard and shapely, or these exquisite small breasts. Her skin also, this richly amber, light molasses skin was impossibly, thrillingly smooth under Laura's lips and her fingertips as she drifted down the girl's incredibly long stomach and belly, pausing frequently to kiss and nuzzle Shontay's delightfully perfect flesh. Anybody who doesn't want to fuck this delicious girl every day is crazy, she thought.

Because they had been fighting, Laura had not yet had a chance to kiss and stroke this marvelous flesh, and now that Shontay had finally yielded to her, apparently having released much of her anger and feelings of rejection for the moment, Laura could indulge her desire to the fullest. She began by descending slowly, kissing the velvety skin of Shontay's taut midriff, letting her lips skim the light, invisible down that rose in infinitesimal soft filaments from it, then pausing at Shontay's deep navel to toy briefly with her in this sensitive region.

But instead of continuing down, she let her lips and hands travel up again to Shontay's lovely small breasts, now kissing and tonguing

Shontay's dark caramel nipples tenderly, lovingly, until she heard Shontay beginning to moan softly, and saw her twisting, biting her lip.

"Ohhnnnn! Oh . . . Laura . . . oh god it feels good!"

It felt marvelous to Laura. While she was kissing and sucking Shontay's small, firm breasts, she slid her hands down the girl's long naked back to her hard little buns, cupping one in each palm and digging her fingers into the resilient flesh, about the size of two round grapefruits. She squeezed them and sucked harder on one of Shontay's nipples.

"Ohhhh . . . I love your body," she breathed, moving her mouth over to the other one, sliding one long forefinger up and down the warm, moist crack between Shontay's hard little buns.

"Oh! Oh yes!" Shontay panted, gently but urgently pushing down on Laura's shoulders with her hands, now writhing more uncontrollably. "Oh yes, Laura . . . I need it . . . oh yes . . . I want it."

Now Laura did slide down, down, further, sliding between Shontay's thighs. "I want to taste this pretty pussy so much," she purred to Shontay, spreading the silky jet-black filaments of hair away from the wet, puckered little love chute.

She had tasted it often before but rarely got enough. Even though Shontay's lovely long naked body was a delicious light molasses hue, her small, gaping cunt lips were black as night, and now oily and shiny with flowing nectars, very wet and tongue-tempting. Between the parted inner lips was a squinchy wet pink feast of raw flesh, and Laura immediately slipped her tongue right into the center of it.

"Anngghh!" Shontay groaned, her body stiffening almost immediately, her long, smooth thigh muscles clenching.

Again Laura got her hands on the girl's lovely curved ass, sliding both of them under Shontay's clenching buns and squeezing them again a she tongued and sucked Shontay's wet black cunt lips, then again burrowed her tongue deep into the juicy pink flesh inside them. Shontay, even with Laura's considerable skill and assistance, often did not come quickly, but this time she was apparently on fire. She began keening and whimpering deep in her throat, then actually thrashed around violently on her back as Laura turned up the heat, flogging Shontay's clit with her tongue, sucking it, and roughly squeezing Shontay's ass cheeks at the same time. She pushed her mouth hungrily into Shontay's streaming cunt, mouth-raping it savagely.

"Oh! Oh!" Shontay whimpered. "Oh god! Laura . . . please! Like I did you. Please!"

Laura quickly realized that Shontay wanted the same thing she had given Laura. They had never really got into some of the more devious sexual practices Laura shared with some other girls, but early in their relationship, Laura had given Shontay a piercing, electrifying orgasm by inserting one long forefinger up into her ass just as she was beginning to come, and Shontay had never forgotten it.

"Oh yes . . . baby . . . you can have anything you want," she murmured to Shontay, glancing over at the bed stand, where Shontay had deposited the small magic bottle.

It took her a little quick maneuvering, but in a few seconds, she had it open and spread a little oil on her finger. Then she snapped it back shut, and pushed it down on the bed near her feet, not bothering to take the time to lean back over Shontay's long, jerking legs to reach the table.

"Oh yes . . . hold on, honey, here it comes," she purred, again licking the dewy black petals of Shontay's delicious slit and slithering her tongue between them, while at the same time parting the girl's hard little buns with the fingers of her left hand.

"Ungghhh!" Shontay groaned, her body suddenly leaping in a violent twitch as she felt Laura's long greased forefinger sliding up into her ass. "Oh . . . god!"

"Yes . . ." Laura purred. "Yes . . . yes . . . go for it, honey . . ."

"Oh! Unh! Unh! Oh shit! Oh yes . . . unhhhhhh!"

Now Laura, knowing Shontay was right on the edge, ready to fall over, unleashed all of her passion. Skewering Shontay's ass on her twisting finger, she again assaulted the girl's sweet, festering pussy with her mouth, sucking Shontay's clit sharply, fucking her ass fervently, feeling Shontay's long, stiffening body suddenly shudder in a deep rumble of release.

"Auungghhh!" Shontay roared, flexing so hard that her long, supple body made a huge, awkward flip off the bed, then fell back into it, writhing and squealing as shattering spasms of coming wrenched her. "Iiiieeeennnggghhh! Ungghiiieeeee!" she yelped, again flipping, surging off the mattress, jamming her ass down into Laura's finger, grinding her pussy into Laura's mouth as each succeeding shockwave struck her.

Laura held on. With her free arm looped around one of Shontay's slender, silky thighs, she rocked up and down with Shontay's wild gyrations until they slowly began to weaken, and Shontay's rough, labored breathing became more audible than her wild screams. When her pelvic girdle finally came to rest, Laura could still feel distant rhythmic contractions going on deep inside Shontay's body somewhere. Shontay's soft, sensitive mewling seemed to grow out of the deep hum of ecstasy that still flowed through her slackening body.

"Oh god," she said, half whimpering while looking down at Laura, her face reflecting the stunned feeling that clearly pervaded her flesh. "I think that was the best ever."

Laura was very careful in slowly extracting her finger, watching intense sensations centered in her plundered rectum replace the stunned look on Shontay's face. "Even better than the one upstairs?" she asked softly, smiling.

Now that Laura's finger was completely out, Shontay recovered her composure. She sat up, smiling back sheepishly. "I liked them both."

"Me too. Now, how about that dinner I promised you."

"Do you mind if we just . . . I don't know, snuggle a little first?"

Shontay was very soft and shy and somber, and Laura could not in any way violate this mood. The girl seemed almost sad, more deeply pensive than Laura had ever seen her. Laura's Latin was not strong, but she had taken a course in high school. *Post coitum omne animal triste est.* All animals are sad after fucking, she translated to herself.

In fact, she felt a little sad herself, probably because of the fight, first, and then the sweet fucking here in her bed, the clear and simple determination they both had to please the other. Why should that make me sad? She wondered. I guess because she is seeing it as the change our relationship will now reflect, that this seals it. I sleep with others too, and she will have to bear the hurt.

"I would love to snuggle," Laura whispered, stretching out next to her.

They held one another without speaking for a long time.

"You smell so good," Laura finally broke the silence, burrowing her nose in Shontay's hair.

"You say that to all the girls," Shontay said, but not in a kidding tone.

Laura thought of Sara. True, she had said it to Sara. It was true, too. They both smelled wonderful to her. And very different, for some reason.

"If I keep smelling you, I'm going to want you again," Laura said, ignoring Shontay's comment. "Smelling you makes my pussy get a little buzzy feeling deep inside. You know that?" She ran her fingertip over Shontay's sensual lips before kissing them again. "I'm sorry about your favorite blouse. And that beautiful bra. I hope you'll let me replace them."

Shontay put her own fingertip on Laura's lower lip. "I'm glad you want me, Laura. Nobody ever wanted me the way you do. Nobody ever wanted me enough to rape me, and you've already done it twice." Her eyes were big and round and pale brown, so unusual and hypnotic.

"I can't believe that," Laura whispered, kissing the fingertip warmly, unable to suppress the beginnings of a blush. "You're making me feel guilty. Come on in and help me cook. We're going to wear each other out without some sustenance."

"Why don't we take a bath together instead?" Shontay said, suddenly bright and cheerful, as if the idea had just occurred to her.

"No wonder you're so skinny," Laura teased, poking her in her delectable ribs, wanting to kiss them all over again, and the rest of this long, smooth, light brown body too. "You turn down food at every opportunity."

Shontay's eyes flashed. "I thought you liked my skinny body."

Laura tilted her head. "Compromise, okay? We eat . . . then we bathe . . . and . . . whatever. You're going to wear me out, girl. Didn't you hear me?"

"What's the matter, Laura, getting old?" Shontay said, with an ambiguous wink.

<<O>>

But Shontay had, a few weeks later, due to simple bad luck for Laura, caught Laura leaving her own apartment with Taneesha, Deshona's stunning young niece, in tow, after having fucked the darling girl nearly to shreds all afternoon. Laura knew they both reeked of lascivious bed games. It had been, to put it mildly, an awkward moment. Though she and Shontay had no claims on one another, Laura knew after the intimacy they had shared—a horrific catfight followed by a scorching sexual makeup—that Shontay felt a deep physical awakening caused by Laura and now violated by Laura's clearly randy and ungovernable promiscuity.

From that moment on, Shontay spurned Laura with an icy scorn that made Laura tremble to think that anyone you had shared piercing orgasms with could be so cold. Shontay by now would not even speak to her. She would only scowl at her coldly if their paths crossed at work, sometimes even moving to the other side of the corridor in an aloof and frigid manner, to show that Laura was leprous and untouchable. Her hair was yanked and knotted back behind her head more severely than ever, and she walked stiffly and with military precision, head held high imperiously on her delicious long neck.

Laura, pausing in amazement and mild sorrow at these withering rejections, found herself wondering if she would be craving the girl's body so much if she didn't know what lay underneath those awkward, baggy, even aggressively ugly business suits Shontay wore, having reverted to them after wearing for a while thin, summery dresses that showed off her marvelous café-au-lait skin and long, slender, but thrilling legs. The transformation was simply a return to her previous self, her pre-Laura self, as if all that hot sex and blossoming confidence in her physical appeal had never happened.

Laura also wondered in passing if she didn't feel the fires ignite in her pussy when Shontay marched so stiffly and contemptuously by her because that kind of scornful rejection only fanned the flames of her lust and doubled her determination to break through it. She had done it before in spite of, it seemed, impossible odds.

Since falling hard for Sara, and then getting involved, lamentably, with Dee Dee, Laura had seen less and less of Shontay, and Shontay, being fiercely bright and perceptive, had quickly picked up on Laura's shifting alliances. Even Laura's grief over losing Sara, it was obviously clear to Shontay, did not involve her. Laura wasn't moping because they hadn't slept together for a week. She was instead mooning after some rival, which sent Shontay not into the dumps but into a purple fury that she could barely contain.

Her manner, however, was not to protest or whine or accuse. Instead, she withdrew into an icy contempt, implacable and frosty. As Laura had often reflected in the past, it was Shontay's 'Off with her head!' manner.

Since they worked in totally different spheres of the business, their paths rarely crossed. Occasionally, however, their presence was required at all-management meetings, and during one of stupefying dullness that had been called to review company financial goals, Laura found herself in a good position to gaze at Shontay for about forty-five minutes. Sitting behind a couple of men with broad shoulders, Laura was half-concealed and could admire Shontay unobtrusively, without seeming to stare; just a causal glance now and then.

Shontay was every bit the ice queen that her reputation called for, her head held high, her gaze sharp and imperious, her scowl intimidating. She was also ostentatiously taking notes, scribbling stiffly and conscientiously on a yellow pad in her lap.

Today she wore the off-white, ivory version of her baggy business suit, which hung on her bony frame like ill-cut draperies, the expensive fabric contrasting wildly with the awkward folds and ripples. The contrast of the ivory fabric with her skin, though, was ravishing. After days of rhapsodizing over the sleek, deeply black skin of Charise and Dee Dee, Laura was mildly startled to recall how enchanting she always found the rich pale clover honey hues of Shontay's skin, so richly highlighted by the ivory fabric of her suit jacket.

Her long swan's neck was delectably visible, even more so with her hair bundled up so tightly behind her head, and the shape of her jaw and her exquisite brown ears were just as perfect as they could be. She was really quite lovely, if you knew her as Laura did (naked, Laura thought, cursing herself for this salacious aside), and it was a great mystery why she felt compelled to appear so reserved, crisp, and scornfully distant. While watching her, Laura recalled how once, when they were lying together in bed after vigorously fucking, Shontay had confessed that though she usually seemed very much in control, she was actually 'scared shitless' most of the time.

Laura wondered if she were scared shitless at this moment. Probably not, she realized. Safety in numbers. Shontay, as if she could feel Laura staring, finally toward the end of the meeting whipped her head around nervously. Laura, safe behind her screen formed by the two men in front of her, merely leaned down to adjust her shoe, and successfully evaded this scrutiny.

She did manage deliberately to run into Shontay at the exit of the meeting room, slyly stepping in front of her to prevent her smooth escape.

"Oh . . . hi!" Laura said brightly, gazing up into those mysterious pale brown eyes that always had a hypnotic effect on her. "Long time no see."

Shontay was nearly four inches taller than Laura and could make anyone blanch by staring down from such a height. She scowled and looked like she wanted to flee. Finally, a pinched, noncommittal smile crossed her lips.

"Hello, Laura." She glowered, her light brown eyes flecked with sparks of anger, as if to accuse Laura of blocking her way, which was true.

"I . . . miss . . . our talks," Laura smiled, trying to appear as friendly as possible. Shontay had accused her often of only wanting 'black cunt,' her way of saying Laura was only after her sweet little pussy. And even though Shontay had exquisite skin the rich color of light molasses, her pussy was indeed very black, Laura knew—the lips, at least.

Oh god, Laura thought, Dee Dee had said the same thing. Maybe I'm becoming too obvious, too crude.

Shontay pursed her lips. "Right. See you, Laura."

She slipped around Laura and stalked down the hallway, not looking back. Fortunately, most of the meeting attendees had dispersed by this time, so that no one was nearby to notice this snub. Good thing, Laura reflected. Company headquarters staff were like the inhabitants of a small village when it came to gossip. She watched Shontay disappear, unable to keep her eyes from straying to the woman's marvelous high little rump that yawed and swayed ever so slightly as she walked, that jutted out a little, something not even the loosely hanging swaths of cloth could conceal.

Laura, though temporarily crestfallen, adjusted to this rejection, feeling that Shontay was certainly within her rights. Laura was deeply and painfully in love with Sara still, and whatever attention she could give Shontay would certainly not be what Shontay appeared to require of her.

To take her mind off it, she slept with Shavon a couple of times, and once with Yvette, always such intense experiences that nothing could put them in the shadows. Mercifully, Dee Dee was out of town in Ann Arbor, trying to see if she could get admitted there in the spring to complete her Ph.D. program. (Sara had paid for the trip.) Laura, though still suffering great miseries of rejected love over Sara, had come to a gradual realization that it was probably really over. This made her less reluctant to sleep with Dee Dee, especially since their times together were hot enough to burn up the planet. On the other hand, she could never quite relinquish a belief in the possibility that Sara would come back to her, and then the shit would hit the fan all over again when she found out that Laura had been screwing Dee Dee regularly.

She had absolutely no evidence to back up this belief.

A few days after this meeting in which Laura ogled Shontay from three rows away, and got contemptuously snubbed at the exit door, an obligatory management retreat was announced. It would be held at a resort in Santa Cruz that was especially designed for business meetings, and would occupy three days of the following week.

Being currently unencumbered by relationships, Laura enjoyed driving down alone, trying not to think of Sara, or what unknown faculty members, male or female, Dee Dee might be fucking in Ann Arbor in order to grease the wheels of graduate admissions. I really became wound up with these two beautiful women, didn't I? She realized.

She hummed to herself, her old standby.

I fall in love too easily,
I fall in love too fast,
I fall in love too terribly hard,
For love to ever last . . .

After a while her thoughts deviated to Shontay, whom she knew would also be at this retreat. Oh god, another three days of freezing stares and huffy tossing of the head. Looking at that long smooth neck . . . that pretty little rump. Those hypnotic light brown eyes. Can I stand it? Having her wither me with a glance?

Forcibly, almost as if to get her mind off Shontay and the mixed blessing it would be to be thrown together with her at this retreat, she let her mind drift back to Sara. Now that she was (mostly) convinced they would never be together again, she could indulge her pained and elaborate fantasies to the fullest, imagining what it would be like at this very instant to be pressing her lips to the swollen, dewy black petals of Sara's lovely wet pussy, nuzzling with her nose the silvery pussy ring, letting the tip of her tongue find the little firm nub of clit underneath it, hearing Sara gasp.

This fantasy almost made Laura's heart stop, before filling again with a sharp pain of loss, and she had to tighten her grip on the wheel in order not to veer off the road. I better think of something else.

*I guess I'll have to dream the rest . . .*she hummed again.
If you can't remember the things that we said,
Those nights when my shoulder held your sleepy head,
If you believe that parting's best,
I guess I'll have to dream the rest . . .

At the resort, she got settled in her room and went out to the pool. There would be a group dinner, preceded by a cocktail party, but until then her time was her own. She knew Shontay would not be appearing at the pool—even if she had already arrived—because she was very self-conscious about her 'skinny' figure. Laura, on the other hand, had nothing to hide and even enjoyed the stares she frequently drew. Let them want, let them wonder, she thought, realizing that she sounded a lot like Dee Dee.

After dinner on the second night (the first had passed without incident, and she had only rarely glimpsed Shontay at the party and the dinner), Laura found herself with about five other management employees in the room of the French representative of their company, playing *Trivial Pursuit*. It was a friendly and uproarious game, and she enjoyed herself immensely. On her way back to her room, she stopped by the small lobby shop for a magazine and ran directly into Shontay, who was clutching an issue of *Marie Claire* in her hand and heading for the counter.

"Oh . . . hi," Shontay said, caught by surprise.

"Hi, Shontay," Laura said calmly. She began leafing through a magazine, more as a prop than anything else, just to be doing something, not looking directly at Shontay.

Shontay continued to the counter and paid for her magazine. Laura was right behind her as she left the shop. Shontay looked around.

"I wish we could talk," Laura said softly, though as far as she could tell only resort employees were left in the lobby.

Shontay looked tired and a little distracted. No wonder, Laura thought. Trying to keep up that cold, hostile exterior all day, all the time. Must be a real effort.

"I don't think we have anything to talk about, Laura."

Laura pursed her lips. "Come on, I'll buy you a drink." She pointed with her head toward the bar.

"You know I don't drink. Hardly ever."

Laura smirked at her, teasingly. "This is a retreat. Make an exception. We're supposed to relax. Get to know each other."

"I already know you as well as I want to," Shontay said, her voice cutting, her face sour.

"Ouch." Laura winced visibly. "You're so cold."

Shontay's pale light brown eyes clouded over briefly, as if this conversation were causing her as much distress as it was causing Laura. "I'm tired. I'm going to my room. Good night, Laura."

Not knowing what else to do, Laura watched her walk away, her magazine clutched in a thick roll under one arm. "By the way, how's Willie?" she half-shouted after Shontay, surprised at the way her voice reverberated through the mostly deserted lobby.

It was a little embarrassing, but a quick look around told her that no one had heard. Shontay turned and appeared shocked that anyone would holler at her after her withering comments. She frowned, as if Laura were an unpredictable maniac. Willie was her parents' cat. Her parents had lived in the apartment above Laura's, until Laura had recently moved.

"I . . . miss him," Laura stammered. "Willie and I . . . always got along."

"Willie's fine," Shontay said coldly.

But this mere pause allowed Laura to cross the space between them again. Now she spoke more softly, intimately.

"If you won't have a drink, why don't we sit by the pool for a few minutes? I really would like to talk to you."

"We have nothing to talk about."

Laura let her gaze fall from Shontay's mesmerizing eyes to her sensual lips. If simple civility would not work, she was willing to try veiled sexual invitation. She realized that sex was really the root cause of Shontay's hostility, and yet they had shared so many intense sexual moments, and sweet ones too, that Laura wondered how Shontay could ignore them.

"I just like to be near you," Laura whispered. "Just for a few minutes?"

Shontay shook her head. She turned and began walking away again. This time Laura followed. They reached the place where the wings of the convention center forked, leading to two different corridors of rooms. Laura stopped and watched Shontay go down one. Shontay looked over her shoulder and saw Laura watching her. She came back.

"Are you following me?" Her eyes looked amused as well as angry.

"I . . . I'm sorry," Laura looked down.

There was a long, painful silence. Laura could hear Shontay breathing.

"Hell . . . if you want to talk so much, okay," Shontay finally said. She began walking back in the same direction, toward her room. "Don't you know we shouldn't be seen having a quarrel like this? Somebody might see us and think we're . . . you know, closer than we are."

Laura followed her without a word. Why is she doing this, she wondered. Why is she inviting me in, after being so cold and mean? Shontay opened the door with her key but paused, turning to Laura.

"Only for a few minutes. Nothing's happening."

"I know. I promise. Just a few minutes."

After turning on the bright overhead light to completely illuminate the darkened room, Shontay turned on the small, dimmer light by the bed, then switched off the first one. She tossed her magazine on the bed and sat down next to it, since there was only one chair. Laura sat in it.

Shontay's face was blank, expressionless. She almost glowered at Laura, waiting for her to begin.

"You wanted to talk."

Laura squirmed. She clasped her hands and rubbed them together awkwardly. "I . . . think I just wanted to be near you. For a few minutes. Without you glowering at me."

Shontay gave Laura one of her patented, pinched smiles. "How's this?"

"I want to kiss you," Laura said, so softly that both of them could barely hear her.

"Laura, you are such a cunt."

"What a thing to say," Laura teased, with a long face. "I made you pant. I made you quiver."

Shontay nodded seriously. "I can do without it."

Laura raised one eyebrow and shrugged. She started to get up. "I can't force you."

"You don't have to go yet," Shontay said, without moving.

Laura sat back. "I don't?"

Shontay shook her head. "Tell me what you think of the meeting."

They discussed the meeting for a few minutes, though Laura was very guarded and noncommittal. Shontay seemed to be fishing, but not too hard. She smoked, opening the window wide to let out the smoke.

"I'm not supposed to smoke in here. It's a non-smoking room."

Laura knew that Shontay smoked when she got nervous. She smoked two cigarettes in a row.

"May I kiss you now?" Laura whispered, getting up from the chair, as Shontay snubbed out the second cigarette.

Shontay seemed paralyzed, her pale brown eyes pulsing as she looked up at Laura coming across the small room. There was no sign on her face of the implacable hostility that earlier had been there. Still, she shook her head. Laura stopped.

"No kissing." She turned her cheek to the side to deflect Laura's kiss, which grazed her cheekbone instead.

Laura pulled back. "Sorry. I thought . . . since we're both forced to be here at this cruddy meeting, we might comfort each other a little."

Shontay gave her a sharp look. "You don't like the meeting? You were lying earlier?"

Laura shrugged. "I never said I liked it."

"I'm on the planning committee for this off-site," Shontay said, sounding wounded. "Tell me what you don't like about it."

"I'd rather not," Laura said, trying to kiss her again.

"Cut it out!" Shontay scooted to the side. "What are you going to do, rape me? Isn't that what you do every time I see you?"

Laura smiled understandingly. "I didn't think you objected. Before."

"I object now. Maybe you'd better go."

"Shontay, you're very lovely. May I take your hair down? You always look so sexy with your hair down. It makes me just . . . quiver inside. Turn your head, and I'll take your hair down for you."

"Don't you touch me!"

Now Laura believed she meant it. Shontay was shaking with fury. Laura backed off. "Okay . . . okay. I know when I'm not wanted."

She pulled back, still standing, not really knowing what to do. Shontay looked completely discombobulated and did not stand up for a few seconds. When she did, she strode in just two steps to the door, her legs being very long and the room very small. Laura looked at her sadly.

But Shontay herself was apologizing as she held the door open for Laura. "I'm sorry . . . it just didn't work out," she mumbled.

Laura paused, half in the door and half out. She whispered, not wanting any stray passerby in the hallway to hear her. "I'm sorry you feel the way you do."

She raised one finger to Shontay's cheek and caressed it, slowly, meaningfully. Then she turned and walked down the dark corridor to the fork, then up the other wing to her own room. She did not know if Shontay was watching her as she walked away, but she did not hear the door shut.

Back in her own room, she showered, then turned on the TV, sound down low, to distract herself. She must have nodded off briefly, for she was awakened by a soft rapping at her door. She crossed the room and opened it a crack, leaving the brass chain fastened.

"Shontay." Quickly, Laura unfastened the chain. "How did you find my room?"

"Are you going to let me in?" Shontay snapped, under her breath.

"Of course."

Laura opened the door, and Shontay slipped inside. Laura's heart had started thumping inside her chest when she noticed that Shontay had taken her hair down. It hung in disheveled clumps around her ears and cheeks. She was wearing a cream-colored terry cloth bathrobe that made her honey-hued skin more beautiful than ever.

"I . . . peeked," Shontay confessed, looking briefly at the floor in embarrassment. "When you left . . . I walked behind you and peeked down the hall. To see which one you went into."

Since Laura did not dare to say anything else at the moment, she closed the door and refastened the chain. Both of them watched her fingers, as if it were a significant gesture, resonating with sexual overtones, the mere slipping of a knob of metal into a slot. Laura turned off the TV. She looked at Shontay, who seemed petrified.

Calm down, honey, Laura said with her eyes, still not daring to speak. We've done this before. Remember?

They were both still standing, only inches apart, since Laura's room was as small as Shontay's. Laura crossed the remaining distance, looking up, since Shontay was so tall.

"Ready for that kiss now?"

Shontay didn't say anything. She didn't move away, either. "I . . . was sorry you left," she whispered. "I'm sorry I made you leave."

"There's nothing for anyone to be sorry about," Laura murmured, uptilting her mouth to Shontay's, trying to beckon Shontay to lower hers a little, since their lips were still inches apart.

"Maybe I should go," Shontay said, suddenly.

This, Laura knew, was a way of acknowledging that if she stayed, they would fuck. Laura smiled at her gently. Shontay was always so skittish, like a thoroughbred.

"I'd be very unhappy if you did," Laura said.

Now Shontay's pale, light brown eyes swam with sexual meanings that she could not suppress. "Okay, then," she said, very softly. "I'm ready."

To make it special, Laura raised both hands to her face, luxuriating in the feel of Shontay's hair brushing her fingers, swinging loose around her cheeks, and pulled Shontay's mouth gently down into hers. A thrilling electric charge coursed through both of them as their lips met, a scintillating current born of their estrangement, the time that had elapsed since they had last done this, and their evasive circling since then.

Shontay's mouth was warm and sensual, and Laura's lips curved into hers slowly, with agonizing sensitivity, before their tongues even met. She was in no hurry and wanted to enjoy every micro-second of this to the fullest. Finally, Shontay's teeth parted, and Laura's tongue slithered inside her mouth, probing, dancing, exploring the entire warm wet cavity, coiling with Shontay's tongue now. She still held Shontay's face in both hands. Shontay was soft and yielding, so different from her earlier sharp, hostile manner. She yielded her mouth to Laura's, letting Laura's tongue fuck her mouth without any counter aggression, until finally the fire inside grew too hot and she began to kiss Laura back more hungrily.

Now Laura was forced into the passive role as Shontay drove her tongue deep into her mouth. Shontay clutched Laura's body through Laura's thin housecoat, and Laura dropped her own hands, finding the sash of Shontay's bathrobe and pulling it loose. She slipped her hands inside, clasping the girl's warm, lean, naked body.

Shontay had a long, supple back that was just a dream of rapture for Laura, who ran her fingers all over it, feeling the long smooth muscles that ran the length of it from her shapely shoulder blades all the way down to her dimpled sacrum.

"I love your back," Laura whispered, momentarily disentangling her tongue from Shontay's, panting. "I want to kiss it all over . . . god, what a beautiful back."

She swept her hands forward as Shontay began kissing her again, pulling them up to Shontay's enchanting small breasts, the size of delicate teacups. Anyone who did not know Shontay's body well, as Laura did, would have been surprised to find them there since in most of her clothes Shontay looked severely flat-chested. But in fact, she had these marvelous, perfect little globes, firm and round, capped by thick, dark caramel nipples that Laura was now pinching gently, insistently.

Shontay pulled back from kissing Laura long enough to smile. "You like those too, don't you?" she panted, her lips wet with Laura's saliva, her eyes shiny and hot.

It had taken her a long time to get to the point where she could enjoy Laura's adoration of her naked body. Shontay was very tall and thin, even skinny, some would say, with thin thighs and marvelously etched bone structure, prominent collarbones, rounded but also slightly bony shoulders. Her ribcage protruded slightly, and her elbows and knees were occasionally a little awkward. But she had a model's body, and certainly a model's face, when she let her hair down, and once you got used to the length of her body and its angles, you could easily become enraptured by it, Laura knew. This rapture of Laura's was almost the sole cause of Shontay's becoming prouder of her physical charms. And ever since that had occurred, she had loved teasing Laura about Laura's hunger for them.

"Tell me how you love my titties," she whispered in Laura's ear, her fingers now scrabbling for the buttons on Laura's housecoat.

"I could eat them for breakfast, lunch and dinner," Laura murmured, pulling open the bathrobe now, squeezing the marvelous small globes. "I could suck them in my sleep."

"Ooooohhhhh," Shontay giggled softly, "you're awake now."

"Oh, I can suck them when I'm awake too."

Laura dropped her mouth to Shontay's breasts, holding them in her hands and peppering them with hot kisses, enchanted by seeing more and more of Shontay's rich honey velvet skin come into view. In the dim light of her room it glowed with a fine sheen like light molasses, and Laura extended her tongue, licking wide swoops around Shontay's glimmering caramel nipples, then letting her lips approach closer to one while Shontay looked down at her mouth.

"Ahhh!" she gasped as Laura sucked the shiny, soft caramel bud inside.

Laura sucked it gently at first, swirling her tongue all around Shontay's nipple and feeling it grow thicker and pulpier inside her wet mouth. Shontay stroked Laura's head, whimpering softly, watching. The harder her nipple became in Laura's mouth, the harder Laura sucked it, until Shontay was moaning and trembling.

"Oh shit . . . I've got to lie down, Laura," she gasped. "You're making my legs weak. God, you do that so well!"

"Quick, lie down on the bed," Laura murmured. "Here, take this off."

Shontay was pliant and obedient, so different from her earlier self, slipping the bathrobe off her body with Laura's help. Laura was quickly out of her housecoat too, and she pulled the bed coverings down, exposing the sheet, in one rapid motion.

"We'll have to be very quiet," she whispered to Shontay, as they stretched out facing one another.

Shontay's pale brown eyes were wide and shiny. She nodded. "I know."

Laura gazed deep into them, hypnotized as usual by their odd sexual power over her. "Now give me that other lovely little breast," she breathed.

Shontay, half-embarrassed but saucy at the same time, cupped her other breast in one hand, looking down, offering it to Laura. "You can do it a little harder, if you want," she murmured.

"Mmmm, does it make your pretty pussy wet when I suck you hard?" Laura asked, quickly taking Shontay's other nipple into her mouth, laving it fervidly with her tongue.

"Oh god, yes!" Shontay whimpered again.

Laura smiled up at her, holding Shontay's wet, erect, caramel nipple playfully between her teeth. She released it momentarily. "Can I see how wet it is?"

The same half-embarrassed but sexually excited grin passed across Shontay's face. She nodded.

But Laura was unwilling to leave Shontay's marvelous small breasts just yet and resumed sucking the wet, pointing nipple she had just released, then returned to the first one, mouth-mauling it passionately now. Shontay squirmed. Her fingers fluttered in Laura's hair, and she arched her back a little, pushing her wet nipples into Laura's face.

"Now . . . let me see," Laura teased softly. "Should I see how wet it is with my finger . . . or my tongue?"

Shontay giggled and panted nervously. "Either one."

"Which do you like the most?"

"Tongue."

"Mmmm . . . it's a long way down this long, beautiful body," Laura purred, now descending, her lips moving skillfully across Shontay's long, palpitating stomach, kissing it everywhere.

"Oh Laura . . ."

Now that she had Shontay in her bed, Laura was in no rush. Though many may have thought Shontay's naked body to be overly angular, bony, and thin, Laura found it enchanting. Shontay's honey-gold skin was covered with a fine, silky down that Laura reveled in rubbing her cheek against, and she could feel the fine silk under her sensitive lips as they inched slowly down the taut, heaving muscles of the girl's very long midriff.

She had to pause for a few seconds at the glistening, raven-black curls of Shontay's small pubic patch of hair, nuzzling the sparkly filaments with her nose, letting the ripe perfumes of Shontay's aroused cunt drift up to her nostrils. She had not tasted this exquisite pussy for weeks, maybe almost two months by now, and she recognized a sharp, sudden hunger in herself for it.

Unlike the rest of her body—long arms, long legs, long torso, long neck, everything very long—Shontay's beautiful pussy was a small treasure, a juicy little wet magenta slot enclosed by glossy black cunt lips that were now gaping and swollen. At the top, presently concealed, was, Laura knew, a tiny but very sensitive clit that she loved to coax out with her tongue, while feeling Shontay's body twinge and clench in fierce anticipation of the climax she often had some difficulty reaching.

"Oh honey," Laura murmured, kissing the smooth, warm inner skin of Shontay's slender thighs, "this pussy is so wet for me. I'll bet you want me to kiss it . . . and lick it . . . as much as I want to."

"Unhhh! Oh . . . yes . . ." Shontay gasped, twisting, looking down her long, thin, undulating body at Laura crouched between her thighs.

"Too bad we have to be so quiet," Laura murmured. "I'd love to suck this beautiful pussy until you scream."

"Oh god . . . we can't make any noise!" Shontay keened, suddenly panicking. "If anyone knew we were doing this . . . oh god!"

It was true. They were very vulnerable to being overheard. It wasn't as if total strangers inhabited all the other rooms along this corridor. They were fellow workers, 'colleagues,' supervisors and vice presidents. To overhear two of their number lecherously rutting in the next room, gasping and squealing and shuddering through the beautiful, intense orgasms Laura and Shontay were capable of giving each other, would be a source of endless amusement and salacious gossip for years to come.

Moreover, Shontay, being an executive director, had much more to lose than Laura did. She also had a hard crust exterior she showed constantly to the world, which she was clearly not eager to have penetrated. Finally, the fact that they were having a torrid lesbian encounter could not fail to raise eyebrows and cause months of prurient titillation.

"Don't worry," Laura smiled up at her reassuringly, parting Shontay's wet pussy lips with the fingers of both hands, exposing the glistening magenta flesh inside. "I'm going to make you come so softly you won't even know it's happening until it's over. Just grab one of those pillows if you feel like moaning too loud, okay?"

Looking like a frightened animal—but also a beautiful woman consumed by fierce sexual excitement—Shontay nodded. She reached one long arm up behind her and pulled down one of the pillows, leaving it close to her head.

In truth, though, Laura was wondering too how she could make Shontay come without unleashing a gusher of helpless moans and shrieks. Shontay was one of those women who did not come easily. She required absolute concentration and focus, and very great patience from Laura, to get to the finish line, and often by the time she got there her physical tension was so supreme that when her climax finally erupted, there was no way she could restrain her piercing cries.

But even though it was daunting, Laura wasn't going to let that stop her. It had taken a lot of anguish on both sides to reach this point in their relationship, and now that Shontay had surrendered once again after an initial resistance, Laura was not about to spurn the offer of this beautiful, long, angular body, or the sweet, sensitive, vulnerable girl who was offering it.

Holding Shontay's small, slick, oozing pussy open with her thumbs, she began slowly to lick the wet, exposed, inflamed cleft sensually with her tongue, starting at the bottom and ending at the top by wriggling the tip of her tongue up under the little hood that sheltered Shontay's tiny clit.

"Oh! Oh!" Shontay gasped, her pelvis jerking up excitedly. "God . . . I don't think I can be quiet!"

"Mmmm, yes you can," Laura purred, now burrowing her tongue into the juicy warm pit. "Just tell me if it gets too intense . . . then I'll slow down."

"Oh! I don't want you to slow down! It feels so good!"

For the next two or three minutes Laura was very careful and Shontay very silent, though the sexual tension was building gradually and relentlessly. Laura did not want it to go too fast, and Shontay was incapable of exploding without warning anyway. Often she shook and strained and mewled for several minutes before erupting. She quivered and mewled almost inaudibly while Laura luxuriated in the opportunity to lick her beautiful wet quim to her heart's content. Finally, Shontay's clit began to swell and become more visible, and Laura could not keep her tongue from sliding over it too.

"Oh!" Shontay gasped, her body clenching now more frequently. "Ohhnnnn!"

Laura found herself recalling her old apartment, and how she had struggled countless times to keep the neighbors from overhearing her cries and those of her climaxing lovers. The last neighbors upstairs, whom she had taken pains to guard from these ecstatic screams, were Shontay's own parents, though they had always been gone when Laura and Shontay had fucked, often heatedly, once after a ferocious cat fight, fucking savagely and sweetly on the floor in Shontay's own parents' apartment. It was hard not to remember it all now as she patiently, carefully, tenderly, then more passionately, licked the wet, shiny, bright magenta insides of the lovely, complicated girl's gorgeous, small, festering pussy, bringing low, guttural moans of pleasure from deep in Shontay's chest.

"Unnhhhh . . . unhhhh . . . unhhhhh Laura . . . ohnnnnn!"

"You're going to come . . . you're going to come, aren't you . . . darling . . ." Laura murmured to her, not really knowing if she was yet, since you never knew with Shontay until it actually arrived, but hoping to encourage her, build her confidence, get her to the pinnacle by cheering her on.

"Oh yes . . . oh yes!" Shontay whimpered, twisting, her beautiful, thin, honey-gold, long body writhing and her small breasts sliding up and down on her chest.

"You missed me, didn't you . . ." Laura chuckled softly. "You missed me sucking and licking your pretty pussy like this, didn't you?"

By now Laura was being much more adventurous, sucking Shontay's clit, hood and all, into her mouth, swirling her tongue around it, kneading Shontay's pretty, smooth little buns with her fingers.

Shontay's body suddenly clenched in a noticeable spasm, and she immediately began churning and panting faster. "Oh god, I think I *am* going to come, Laura! Yes! Oh shit . . . right there! Yes! Right there! Ungghh!"

Laura wanted her to come, but the closer they got, the more frightened she became of the consequences. It was a terrible dilemma. She wanted to pour it on about now, to give Shontay what she really needed to reach an obliterating orgasm of the kind Laura had given her countless times in the past. Shontay had become almost addicted to the way Laura often slid one long forefinger up into her ass just before she came, igniting exuberant firestorms of coming in a girl who had known nothing but her own tame, masturbatory orgasms before Laura came into her life. She craved it and would beg for it. It was, Laura reflected, about as kinky as they had ever become together.

Shontay was close to losing all control, and yet Laura, who knew she couldn't risk the finger-up-the-ass this time—it was way too dangerous—could not resist slipping one of her fingers between Shontay's smooth, tight little buns and pressing her fingertip against Shontay's perineum, the small area of skin between the lower part of her cunt and her asshole, a very sensitive spot, Laura knew.

"Ahnnggmmiiee!" Shontay cried out, her body almost jackknifing at the touch, her cry much louder than anything Laura had elicited from her so far.

"The pillow, honey . . . the pillow," Laura coached her softly, reaching up with her free hand and pulling it closer to Shontay's face, which was already torn by a grimace of piercing sexual feeling.

"Oh . . . oh yes! Unhhhhh!" Shontay panted, now swirling her hips, pushing her pussy up into Laura's mouth.

This was, to Laura, a very good sign. She's close. She is going to make it . . . any second. Now Laura began to massage Shontay's perineum while sucking and tonguing her pussy even more heatedly, though well aware that any instant she might have to take quick measures to muffle the girl's helpless screams as Shontay's long body began undulating more rapidly, and her breathing became more labored.

"Yes, honey . . . yes, honey . . . I'm going to suck your beautiful pussy so hard . . . you're going to come so hard . . . I'm going to fuck you so hard . . ." Laura murmured, knowing also that even though she would deny it, Shontay got aroused by having Laura talk dirty to her while fucking her.

Now Shontay began straining, and small, tortured, cawing sounds fought their way of her throat as her flesh clenched and stiffened. Laura had seen this before and was briefly discouraged. Often Shontay would nearly come and then for some reason fall back, as if getting to the peak were something she could not permit herself, as if there were obstacles that even she could not overcome.

But Laura had helped her overcome them dozens of times in the past, and now she only redoubled her efforts, half-gratified anyway that it wasn't going to end too soon, that she still had plenty of time to slurp this delicious small wet black pussy she was so hungrily devouring. The warm, thick nectars that flowed from Shontay's inflamed slit were tangy and tart and sweet and buttery all at once, and Laura drank them, grunting and snuffling almost comically herself with fervent lust as she rubbed Shontay between her anus and her pussy more and more insistently, and lashed Shontay's nearly-bursting clit with her tongue.

"Ungghh . . . ungghhh!" Shontay groaned, tossed her head, her body again jerking upward at the feel of Laura's finger pushing ever more sharply against her perineum.

"Oh yes . . . it's coming, honey . . ." Laura panted to her, sucking her clit, swallowing her sweet juices, now so in tune with Shontay's surging, pulsating flesh that she actually could feel the moment when Shontay finally arrived. "Oh god . . . it's now, baby!"

She didn't need to tell Shontay. Fortunately for them both, the first lightning bolt of Shontay's orgasm struck her so severely that the breath totally left her lungs. Only a tiny, hysterical squeaking could escape from her throat as her long, gangly body stiffened and then collapsed in spasms. This momentary silence gave Laura the opportunity to slide up Shontay's body, while replacing her tongue with her finger, thrusting it up into Shontay's clasping pussy and fucking her rapidly with it, as she covered Shontay's mouth with her other hand and held her, hearing the cries explode from deep in her chest.

"Awwoommmnnnnggg!" Shontay groaned loudly into Laura's palm, her body jumping and straining as each fresh spasm wracked her. "Unnggmmm!"

A wrenching, crushing orgasm roiled inside her, and she lay twitching and shuddering through it for almost half a minute. Laura held her and kissed her smooth cheek and waited. Finally, it began to release its grip on her.

Laura was briefly alarmed that Shontay's cries were too loud, but before she could grab the pillow and turn Shontay's face into it, they began to subside into long, tremulous sighs of pleasure. The undulations of her body began to slow too, and the fluttering of her eyelids grew still. Laura held her, removing her hand from Shontay's mouth now, but still gently moving her fingers inside the warm, greasy folds of Shontay's still-throbbing pussy, unwilling to let the smallest twinge of pleasure die away.

After a few seconds of truly intense moaning and thrashing together on the bed, they were silent. The room was silent. It was quiet enough to hear their breathing, slowly returning to normal. It seemed like an eternity to Laura before Shontay turned her head and smiled wanly, her magical pale brown eyes still pulsing with the afterglow of this thrilling climax.

"I don't care how much you hurt me, I guess I'll always come back," she confessed in a hushed voice. "I don't think I could ever come like that in my life unless you did it."

"What a thing to say," Laura teased, acting mildly shocked. She wiggled her finger inside Shontay's warm pussy and watched Shontay's magical eyes roll up briefly. "One, I never tried to hurt you. Two, you might come even better with someone else, if you tried it."

Shontay shook her head solemnly. "I don't think so. And you do hurt me. You hurt me when you ignore me."

This was unpleasant information, though Laura could hardly act as if she didn't already know it. She was already so aroused from bringing Shontay to a stupendous orgasm and trying to make sure they weren't overheard that her mind could barely concentrate on Shontay's so typical complaints.

"I . . . I've been . . . very distracted lately," she stammered apologetically. "I . . . got hurt very badly myself."

At first Shontay looked curious, then pained. "Welcome to the club," she smirked, unable to repress a smile as she said it.

Laura removed her fingers reluctantly from the girl's warm, buttery slit. Shontay instantly recoiled.

"Don't touch me with that shit!" she half-giggled, trying to pull away, though Laura wouldn't let her. "Eeeewwooo . . . you're fingers are all wet!"

Laura smiled in wonder. She couldn't get over the squeamishness some women had about their own love juices. "You made it," she teased Shontay, glad to have a reason to change the subject. She waved her shiny wet fingers in Shontay's face, threatening to touch her with them. "It's your pussy juice. I love it. Watch."

Sensually, she wrapped her tongue around her two fingers and licked them clean.

"Yum. You have a delicious pussy, my dear. Why are you so afraid of this yummy nectar?"

Shontay frowned at her playfully. "Since you like it so much, you can have it all."

Laura was still holding her close, preventing her escape with one arm. She wiped the spittle off her fingers on the edge of the sheet. Then, turning to her most sultry, submissive manner, she cuddled closer to Shontay.

"Make love to me, honey," she whispered. "Make love to me. Make me come. Just put your hand down there and let me kiss you while I'm coming so I don't scream."

Shontay softened. A tiny smile again tugged at the corners of her mouth. Her pale brown eyes suddenly swirled with flecks of scintillating sexual fire.

"You sure?" she murmured, bringing one hand up to Laura's naked breasts, caressing and squeezing them, twisting Laura's nipples gently in her thumb and forefinger. "You don't want me to eat your pussy? You have a pretty nice one too, you know."

"I do want you to," Laura nodded. "But I want to kiss you and look into your eyes. I want you to look into mine and rub me and make me come. You can eat me when we get home."

"Mmmm," Shontay half-purred, dropping her mouth now to Laura's nipples, teasing and licking them. "Who said we're going to do this again when we get home?"

Laura didn't want to answer. She didn't want anything to get in the way of this pleasure, which seemed to grow and swell by the second. For all their checkered relationship and mutual suspicion, she and Shontay had been making love for months, and Shontay knew what it took to ring Laura's bells. Her mouth on Laura's breasts had Laura climbing the walls very quickly.

"Oh . . . god, that feels good!" Laura breathed, looking down at Shontay's wet, pink tongue dancing over her stiffening coral-hued nipples.

Shontay sucked each one slowly, skillfully, passionately, stopping only when Laura began lowing and groaning softly, twisting, pushing her pelvis forward into Shontay's body, giving every indication that she would not last much longer and desperately needed Shontay to bring her off.

"Oh god, you're killing me, I need it . . . I need it!" she whimpered into Shontay's hair, again delighting in the way it fell in messy, sexy clumps around Shontay's cheeks and forehead.

Shontay lifted her head, smiling, still massaging Laura's saliva-wet breasts with her fingers, now scissoring Laura's erect nipples between her long slim fingers. "I wish I could come as fast as you do," she whispered, her light brown eyes swirling, pulsing.

The sexual spell they had cast together now swept away Shontay's resentments, and she was totally caught up in the heat of the moment, as Laura was.

"Kiss me, you idiot," Laura panted, half-smiling. "You sex maniac. You rapist. Kiss me and fuck me with your hand."

Shontay's magical pale eyes flickered with mischief. "What if I don't?"

"Oh god, please," Laura panted, her face contorted by fierce need.

"Mmmm, I love you to beg me," Shontay said, kissing Laura's neck, breathing in her ear, sliding one long, graceful hand down Laura's body to her crotch, which was so hot and wet it was nearly steaming.

"Unhhhhh!" Laura gasped as she felt Shontay slide two fingers up into her squinchy wet furrow.

Shontay pulled her face out of Laura's hair. "You smell so good, Laura," she whispered, her breath now coming faster too. She looked seriously, almost solemnly, into Laura's eyes. "You've got to be quiet too."

"Oh! Oh! Oh god . . . it feels so good . . . just like that, yes!"

Laura began to gyrate her hips in slow, sensual fuck-rhythm, feeling Shontay's long slender fingers slide in and out of her sopping wet pussy. Shontay knew the effect her hand was having on Laura, and she was quickly drawn into the whirling vortex of Laura's gathering need, moving her fingers faster, letting the bottoms of them slide across the throbbing nub of Laura's clit, even clutching Laura's body harder against hers with her other arm.

"Laura . . ." she panted, now fucking Laura's pussy so hard and squirming together with her that the bed began to squeak. "You can't make any noise!"

"I know!" Laura gasped, pressing the full length of her body into Shontay's warm flesh, feeling her damp nipples slide against Shotnay's stiff little buds, jamming her crotch down into the girl's thrusting hand. "Unhhh! Ungghh! Oh!"

"Laura!"

"Auunngghh!"

"Laura . . . the pillow! Here!"

For all her concern about protecting them from the consequences of Shontay's potentially loud orgasm, Laura when it came to her own seemed to lose complete control. She knew it was dangerous, she knew she must control her moans and her cries, but somehow the moment—this delicious connection with Shontay in her bed after so much pain over Sara and so much distress at feeling Shontay's rejection—was piercing and sweet and overwhelming all in the same instant. She wanted to scream with joy as she felt the hot, rushing jolt of a surging orgasm begin to fill her body.

"Here!" Shontay almost shouted again, snatching the pillow that Laura had earlier pulled close for her to use, and pushing it into Laura's face, forcing it between them, just as an ear-splitting, helpless cry of thrilling rapture ripped its way out of Laura's throat.

"Owwmmmnngggwwoommmmmoouunngghh!"   Laura screamed into the pillow, her body stiffening, then collapsing into several sharp spasms as a stirring orgasm wracked her. "Unnmmmgghh . . . ohngghhh!"

After a few seconds, she turned her face aside from the pillow to breathe as the intensity weakened, and her moans grew correspondingly softer. Her hips were still undulating and quivering, and she could still feel Shontay's two fingers sunk deep inside her pussy, and Shontay's long arm wrapped around her back, pulling her close. As Laura's groans subsided into panting, Shontay pulled the pillow away.

"You didn't get to look in my eyes, like you wanted," she whispered, kissing Laura's cheek. "You can look in them now."

"Oh god, I think I could have another one, if you just hold it like that!" Laura gasped, knowing with some mysterious certainty that she was poised on the edge of a second climax.

Looking into Shontay's pale eyes, so adoring, so soft, smoldering with so much sex and affection and sensuality, made it even more certain.

"Are you really going to come again?" Shontay asked softly, as if unbelieving.

"I . . . think so," Laura panted, again pushing her throbbing pussy down into Shotnay's hand. "Look at me . . . look at me . . . and fuck me . . ."

"Like this?"

"Oh god, yes! Unhhhh! Oh god . . . yes, right now . . . it's—"

This time she was not so afraid of screaming and merely pushed her face into Shontay's smooth shoulder, squeaking and mewling as a fresh orgasm streamed through her body like a radiant wave, filling her flesh with warm honey, then melting into small feathery spasms that seemed to last an eternity. Shontay held her throughout, then kissed her gently on the face as Laura began to recover.

"I'm so envious," she murmured, seriously, kissing Laura's forehead, finally removing her fingers from Laura's wet pussy. She wiped them, trying to be surreptitious, on the sheet. "Not only can you come so quick, you can also come twice. Like at the same time. First one, then another. God, I've never done that."

"Did I make too much noise?"

Shontay broke into a grin. "You were trying. I nearly suffocated you with that pillow to get you to stop."

Laura nodded. "You did. I guess it was necessary. I don't know what came over me. Just having you . . . hold me like that, and doing everything to me . . . and I just came and I couldn't help screaming."

Shontay loved this praise and nearly blushed herself, looking down momentarily. "I guess I'm getting it right."

Laura embraced her ardently, and kissed her sensual mouth hungrily. "I guess you are."

They dozed dreamily, nestled together, for a long time. Laura luxuriated in pushing her face into the messy clumps of Shontay's hair, inhaling the clean, somehow sexually stirring, odor of her scalp, and the musky perfume that now seemed to wreathe her skin as the consequence of their sweet coupling. She knew she probably smelled the same way to Shontay.

"I'm beginning to want you again," she murmured drowsily into Shontay's molasses-colored ear, slipping her tongue inside of it.

Shontay giggled softly and squirmed free. "Laura! We can't. It's bad enough we did it already. What if somebody heard? Do you know who's in these rooms next to you?"

Laura shook her head. "We were quiet enough. Don't worry."

Now that she had thought of it again, Shontay seemed very nervous. Laura tried to calm her.

"I want your body," she murmured, kissing Shontay's long, smooth, golden neck. "I want to push my pussy into your pussy."

Shontay squirmed again, this time not so much out of nerves as renewed sexual excitement. "We can't. Wait until we get home."

"You said we might not be doing this when we get home," Laura smiled, feigning petulance, pouting.

Shontay softened. "I can't . . . stop wanting to," she confessed. "I told you . . . I never came that way except with you. I can't stop wanting it."

Even though Shontay looked like she wished she *could* stop wanting it, Laura understood. "Great. Then, when we get home, we have a big fucking party at your place. How about it?"

Shontay frowned. "You're making fun of me."

"Am not," Laura grinned.

"Are too." Shontay cocked an eyebrow. "Why can't we have it at your place? Have you got something to hide?"

"Only the depths of my lust for your wonderful sexy skinny body," Laura laughed, dragging her down on her back on the mattress and swarming all over her in a passionate fever of mock lechery.

They laughed and rolled around tickling one another for about a minute, until the bed began to squeak. Then it seemed to occur to both of them at the same instant that they might be overheard having this tickle mania moment. How ironic to be caught playing when nobody overheard us fucking like two lust-crazed minks only a few minutes ago, Laura thought. She could see from Shontay's eyes, even though her face was contorted with suppressed laughter, that she was thinking the same thing.

They had rarely if ever shared such a relaxed, playful moment. Laura wondered if Shontay had ever shared one with anybody. It brought a new intimacy into their relationship, a deeper emotion that now made them both more reluctant to part. And yet Laura knew in the back of her mind that if she were not feeling so bereft of Sara, she would not be feeling this deep tug of emotion for Shontay.

"I have to go back to my room," Shontay said, sitting up, looking around the room for her bathrobe.

"I wish you would stay here," Laura purred, trying to pull her down to the sheet again. "We could sleep and, you know, cuddle and . . ."

"That's just the problem," Shontay pulled away. "I can't control my feelings." Her eyes sparkled at Laura, and she gave her a small, reluctant grin.

"You mean you want it like I do," Laura said.

Shontay nodded, but in the next moment she got up from the bed, found her bathrobe crumpled on the floor, shook it out, and slipped it on. "I've got to go back. In the morning there will be more people in the halls. They'll see."

"I know," Laura admitted.

It was the right thing to do. She couldn't deny it. She waylaid Shontay at the door. They kissed, softly, romantically.

"I had fun," Shontay whispered.

"Me too," Laura winked. "Sleep tight."

But after Shontay had left, Laura could not sleep herself. Boy, 'fun' doesn't even describe it, she thought. That was intense. She is a very intense woman. I mean, we just diddled a little and each of us came . . . but it was emotionally intense.

She switched on the small TV in the corner and realized after a few minutes that it had been the wrong thing to do. On the old movies channel, *To Have and Have Not* was playing, starring Bogie and Lauren Bacall. Laura recalled Sara having told her that if she had been born white she would want to look like Lauren Bacall. "Sorry, Laura," she had said, with her usual sardonic wit. "You're second."

The memory was piercingly sad to Laura, who sat up watching the movie until one o'clock, trying to pay attention to it without thinking of Sara.

The End

Here is a sample from another story you may enjoy:

HOT LESBIAN EROTICA

La Chatte Noire

THE LAURA AND SHONTAY CHRONICLES, PART 3

Miranda Mars

There was an uncomfortable shock in store for Laura.

She was in ninth heaven after her night with Arthell, which helped to cushion the blow a little, though not much. While lying in bed with Sara on Friday night, in Sara's apartment, tired and happy after an hour of intensely sweet and tender fucking, Sara grew solemn. Tracing an invisible line down Laura's cheek with one finger, her dark eyes wide and limpid, she asked,

"Would you hate me if I did this with another woman?"

When Laura, who was floored by the totally unexpected question, failed to answer right away, Sara went on. She even kissed Laura's mouth, half-open with awe and shock first.

"Don't be shocked," she whispered. "It wouldn't mean I didn't love you. I know how upset you were when Evangelina paid me that visit. Even though she and I are old friends, you see it didn't affect the way I feel about you." Sara's fingertip made a curve under Laura's chin and up her other cheek. "And I know you haven't been exactly... how shall we put it... chaste? I don't mean just Dee Dee. But I'm not blind. I can sense when you've been... you know, sniffing some other chick's crotch."

She made one of her devastatingly funny faces, which, in spite of her stunned silence, made Laura laugh. It was a gesture that made it absolutely impossible for Laura to lie and protest that Sara's accusation was not true. She considered the better part of discretion to remain silent.

But when Sara did not go on, Laura said, "I wouldn't hate you. I would never hate you."

"I hope you mean it," Sara said softly.

"Why. Have you done it already?"

Sara shook her head, looking suddenly very innocent and shocked to be suspected. "Only with Lina. I mean, Evangelina." She propped her head on her hand, gazing intently into Laura's eyes. "There's this nurse who works down at 450 Sutter, across the hall from my office. We meet in the hallways, in the elevator, down at the snack shop, you know. She's been sort of, well, you know, coming on to me. It's kind of getting under my skin, if you know what I mean."

Laura nodded sympathetically, not knowing what else to do. She was both pained and fascinated by Sara's account of this attraction. "And you want to give her the green light? See what happens?"

Wide-eyed, Sara slowly nodded. "She's kind of pretty. Not as gorgeous as you are, but..."

"Is she white or black?" Laura blurted out before she could catch herself. "Or Latina," she quickly added, remembering Evangelina. Or 'Lina,' as Sara had just called her, revealing a level of intimacy that Laura had always expected was there but that hurt just the same when she was reminded of it.

Sara frowned, not a deep frown but a frown nonetheless. "Why? Does that even matter to you?" Then she made a dopey face. "Are you that competitive, Laura?"

Laura blushed. "I... guess I am. Sorry."

"Lucky for you, she's a sister." Sara raised one eyebrow. "Knowing you, she'd probably turn your crank."

"Now that's not nice," Laura smiled. "She obviously turns yours."

Sara smiled mysteriously back at Laura. "I guess in a way she does."

Laura recognized this moment as a time when she could pout and turn petulant, perhaps playing on Sara's clear uneasiness at broaching this question. She decided not to do it. After all, you haven't been a saint, she reminded herself. You love her, and you know fucking with the others hasn't made you love her any less. Why shouldn't it work for her, in spite of the fact that I'm wildly and murderously jealous?

"What's her name?"

"None of your business," Sara turned away, as if to brush off this inquiry quickly.

"You mean I don't even get to know my rival's name?" Laura asked querulously, caressing Sara's bare brown shoulder. She realized she was skirting perilously close to the pouting she had foresworn.

"She is *not* your rival!" Sara said, angrily.

"I know… I'm sorry," Laura said, pulling her down again on the bed, running her hands hungrily all over Sara's wonderful curvaceous body, even though they had finished fucking only minutes earlier.

She realized that Sara's attraction to another woman suddenly made her somehow incredibly more desirable than ever to Laura. Her body felt suddenly new, fresh, and alluringly voluptuous under Laura's fingers. Her scent is outrageously erotic. Her skin is a magnet for Laura's hungry lips. In another second, she had Sara's phenomenal breasts in both hands and was attempting to swallow one of her large, soft black nipples.

If you enjoyed this sample then look for **La Chatte Noire.**

Also by this Author:

Deep Excavation

Chocolate Sandwich

Post-Game Specials

A Breach in the Preacher's Daughter

Deeply Detoured

The Rich Bitch Itch

"Hard" Competition

Little Rich Girls Go First

Superior Playmate

Spicing Up a Business Conference

Green Minds Lead to Colorful Results

Dirty Acquaintance

Menage a Trois

Provisional Test

Holiday Treat and Heat

Sex on the 46th Floor

Sneak, Peek and Squeak

Distance Leads to a Sexual Marathon

Confessions and Steamy Clinches

Screams of Pleasure

Sweet Surrender

A Fine Day for Car-washing

A Reunion to Remember

Lustful Temptations

Love and Pain at the Dentist

Unwanted Visit

Sibling Rivalry

Her Undoing

Ashley's Sister Audrey

Infidelity Strikes

A New Love Nest

Sandwich Shop Seduction

Little Sex Bunny

A Secret Affair

The Girl of My Girl

Consumed By Jealousy

Erotic Explosion

Skylark . . . Have You Anything To Say To Me?

Laura Loves College Girls

Arthell Revisited

Arthell Loves To Kiss

Arthell Doubles Down

There, I've Said It Again...

There's No One But You

There Is No Greater Love

Sex Frenzy

A Rising Star

Raging Desire

It Hurts So Good

I Remember You

Don't Adore Me, Just...

Bittersweet Reunion

And Sheena Makes Three...

Gail's Awakening

We'll Be Together Again

Taneesha Wants Some of That

"Some Say the World Will End in Fire... Some Say in Ice..."

Reckless Betrayal

Please Take Me Back, Baby!

Play Coquette

Pervert Devotion

My Little Yoga Darling

Icicles Can Melt

Caught in the Act

Pull My Hair and Make Me Come!

The Emperor Wants Your Pussy!

Three on a Bed

No One Can Replace You

Lock Up the Dogs!

Not While She's Looking

Blindfold Me and Lick Me All Over

Do Me Up the Ass Please

Ride 'Em Cowgirl

I'm Going to Come So Fast

Gina Loves the Dick

Bathtub Sex With Frankie

Spanking Gina's Beautiful Black Ass

Finding Marni's G-Spot

Naked and Horny in the Woods

Marni Wants It Hard, Ashley Wants It Wet

Water My Ficus

Deshona Chronicles Compilation

Kissing Marni's Mom

Shagging Shamika's Aunt

Laura and Gail Chronicles

Laura and Frankie Chronicles

Laura and Arthell Chronicles Compilation

Laura and Makeeda Chronicles Compilation

Bonnie Chronicles Compilation

Drilling for a Filling

Bi-Curious: A Compilation

Revenge Is So Sweet

Double Or Nothing for Allisha

From the Author

If you'd like to give me comments or suggestions to any of my books, feel free to shoot me an email at:
miranda_mars@awesomeauthors.org.

Check my page on Amazon and my blog for Updates and interesting info.

Author Central - http://amzn.to/14wSFHW
Author Blog - http://miranda-mars.awesomeauthors.org/

If you enjoyed any of my books then please share the love and click like on my books in Amazon.

If you write me a review and send me an email I will send you a free book, or many.
(Just know that these emails are filtered by my publisher.)

Good news is always welcome.

One Last Thing, For Kindle Readers...

When you turn the page, Kindle will give you the opportunity to rate this book and share your thoughts on Facebook and Twitter. If you enjoyed my writings, would you please take a few seconds to let your friends know about it? Because... when they enjoy they will be grateful to you and so will I.

Thank You!

Miranda Mars
Miranda_mars@awesomeauthors.org

About the Author

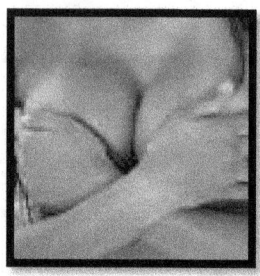

Miranda Mars lives with her cats and her exercise machines with her "special" friend in a suburb in San Francisco. Here is where she lavishly spends scribbling erotica for your, and her own, amusement.

She is especially attracted to dark-skinned women, and uses them as the lovers of the main characters in the stories she writes. She says they're just so hot! So dark-skinned women, BEWARE! :-)

Her stories are also surprisingly VERY ENTERTAINING for MEN!